The Reason the Dress Is Yellow

THE REASON THE DRESS IS YELLOW

Stories

Steve Mitchell

Press 53
Winston-Salem

Press 53, LLC
PO Box 30314
Winston-Salem, NC 27130

First Edition

Copyright © 2024 by Steve Mitchell

Cover art, "Yellow Coat," Copyright © 2012
by Peter Tandlund

Cover design by Kevin Morgan Watson

Library of Congress Control Number
2024939011

ISBN 978-1-950413-83-6

CONTENTS

YIELD

I'm laughing in the fall. Laughing the instant control dissolves, the laughter replacing fear somehow, the laughter a vanishing into space, a lightness, a return.

Emma hears my laugh from below. "You were like a kid," she'd say later. "It was almost a giggle."

I haven't made it very far up the rock face before I realize I can't go back. The ledges are too narrow and spaced too far apart, the sheer walls slick where they've been cut away. I was an idiot to start in the first place, but I'd seen guys scramble their way up before, then leap into the still pool below, and something about the quiet contentment of the day made me brave or adventurous, or simply stupid. Now, I cling to the smooth stone, my feet tensing on a narrow shelf, staring into the forty-foot drop below then tilting upward across sixty feet to the rock ledge above where everyone jumps.

Emma is staring off across the still surface of the water in the center of our picnic blanket. Now and then her gaze turns lazily toward me, and she waves and smiles.

I shift my feet on the shelf, clutching a jut in the rock

with one hand while the other flaps cluelessly in the air. I flatten my body against the stone, then lean out as little as I can to find a path above me, twisting this way and that an inch or so from the wall. The air is calm and silent. I slide my free hand over the face in front of me. It's warm in the strong sun, polished and bright.

It's easier once I accept the situation. I give up looking down, trying to determine how to return; I only look up. I don't think about the ground, I think about the top. I find one handhold then another, inching up an arm's length at a time, balancing my toes on the thinnest slip of rock, my fingers pushing into crevices. Now and then, I come across a tiny stand of grass or a seedling tree clinging to a thin film of collected soil.

I lose my breath twenty feet from the ledge and stop, my feet angled flat against the face, one hand over a crag. My knuckles scraped, my fingertips sore, calves trembling. I rest my cheek against the stone and listen to the surge of my pulse, my chest pushing at the rock until it settles.

The sky is a brilliant blue above the ledge and just before I crest, it's the only thing I can see. I pull myself over the lip and onto the plateau. I lie there for a moment, the loose dirt and gravel sticking to my arms and face, then I roll onto my back, staring into the cloudless sky.

Emma is watching for me when I stand. She applauds, I take a bow. She lies back along the picnic blanket. Her dark skin and red swimsuit against the blanket calling to mind a languishing exotic bug.

There are higher ledges in the quarry—it's impossible to know if anyone has attempted them—but my view is magnificent. The still bowl of the sky and the motionless water. The rose and umber layers of stone exposed in sheer cuts hundreds of feet high.

I brush the grit from my bare knees, drunk on the sense of achievement arcing the surface of my skin, the tips of my tender fingers. It's a clean, blue burn with no thought and no voice; a particular kind of exhilaration I haven't felt since I was a kid. A moment of stillness; the active hum sometimes felt after music ends.

The last notes fade and Emma raises on an elbow from our sprawl in front of my stereo. We'd met at a party, some large, swaggering house party. I was in my fourth year, she was in her third and it was a loud night of drinking, dancing, pushing people into the pool. It's humid and sweaty and we've only just met but we begin to talk, shouting over the music and noise, a conversation that halts and spins with shouts from another room or someone lurching between us and collapsing onto the sofa.

And we talk, until we end up at my apartment, sprawled on the floor before the stereo, a few feet apart. And we listen to *For Emma, Forever Ago*, not speaking at all. We're silent from start to finish because that's why I'd brought her back, and when she raises on her elbow in the stillness after the last note, opening her eyes for the first time since the CD began, her face slick and flushed, I believe I have some glimpse of her secret nature, something definite and mysterious.

The sense of silence changes shape when I reach the edge and look over. My body stutters back from the view, from the possibility of the limitless drop toward the surface, back six feet to the rock wall at the other end of the ledge. There's nowhere to go but up. Or into the water. I know the water is deep enough; I've seen others dive over and over, tanned bodies folding straight, razor clipped, slicing the surface then disappearing for so long I'd wonder if they were coming up again.

I resist the urge to look down the rock face in hopes of finding a hidden traverse invisible before. I back away from the lip as if preparing to race forward and into the void but I'm not going to do that. I know I'm not going to do that. Instead, I make my way toward the ledge, gazing across the quarry toward the blank, opposite wall, then down into the motionless blue surface below.

I inch my bare feet over the edge, the crust of the rock scuffing into the soles, my toes curling over air, until only my heels bind me. But I can't jump. My body won't let me, my muscles contracting away from a leap and hunkering low. I don't look down to Emma, pinned to her blanket far below. I don't look down to the water or over to the opposing face. I can't close my eyes, teetering there on the cliff. I look up, into the empty shell of the sky. After a moment, I do the only thing I can. I lean into the open.

I lean into the kiss. Hoping it is a kiss. Closing my eyes without thinking. Feeling my body tilt forward slowly, my calves tightening, my toes curling. My heart is racing. I can feel the pulse in my palms. There's the strange sensation of the whole of my body at once, as a single arching motion. There's the interval when I've gone too far to stop. I hang there, caught upon some invisible notch in the air. The world narrows to a singular moment and overcomes me. There's no separation, nothing to distinguish the world around me from who I am. We are exactly the same. I move through space in all directions, outward then back again, dragging the world with me, dragging it into me, pulling in as much as I can just before gravity takes me.

Closing my eyes, I follow a narrow thread of warmth to the glance of her skin then the damp exhaustion of her body shading toward mine and our lips find each other. I open my eyes, hers are open too, and we don't speak, we follow the rhythm our lips dictate, slow and soft, a caress diligently finding itself. It's something we watch from a slight distance as it gathers shape before us, our bodies balancing at the point of contact like a pendulum magically arrested in its widest arc.

Emma's hand comes to my face, the back of her hand warm on my cheek, and I lean further in, my hand rising from the floor to her bare shoulder. She tilts her head, lowering imperceptibly. I press my lips to hers. I feel her breath on my skin, the beer, the coffee, the chips, and something deeper at the base of her neck. My hand slips between her shoulder blades and her body gathers around it. I slide closer. She relaxes into my hand and we drift for a moment before she folds and I fold with her.

I arch into the open space. My toes leave the ledge, thrusting away at the last instant.

"You fell asleep," I kidded her, years later. "The end of our first kiss and you were dead asleep."

She chuckled, her hand snaking through the bedclothes to find mine. "I remember your arms around me, the last lines of that song. That's all. What was it, four in the morning?"

"Something like that."

"You were so sweet that night. Gentle, like you'd nearly vanished. When I woke up in your bed the next day, I wasn't frightened or nervous at all."

We were cocooned in our morning warmth, our legs and arms sliding over each other as we delayed the moment of leaving the bed. I turned toward her, eyes glazed with sleep.

"Terror," I told her. "That's all it was. I couldn't catch my breath. I'd close my eyes now and then, just so I knew where I was."

I'm standing at the foot of the bed. I don't know what to do with my hands. Afraid to move, I let others rush around me. It's a moment between breaths, extending to the instant Emma looks up to me, propped finally on the pillows, her hair damp, sweat trickling from her chin, her face radiant. The moment she looks up to me and gently calls me over.

"Johnny, come and see."

And Maggie is there, quiet against her breast, her face finding itself after the effort of birth. Wisps of hair slicked to her head, eyes closed, tiny lips whispering.

Emma lifts her hand and I take it, sliding onto the bed beside her. She's blazing, heat baking off in red waves, rising into my face and cradling the baby.

I can't tear my eyes from Maggie. Her tiny fingers curling and clutching at the air, her tender cooing sounds. She finds her shape along Emma's body, fingers pawing gently at skin, legs pumping beneath the thin blanket, lips working out a new language.

Emma drops her damp cheek to my shoulder and her body follows, her weight collapsing into mine, her heat pushing through my clothes. I can't make out anything past the edge of the bed. The room is very far away. Emma calls my name again, softly, but I can't turn to her; I can't move at all.

"She's. . ."

Maggie opens her eyes. Her irises a deep blue, her huge pupils gray and translucent pools. She opens her eyes into mine and I flicker out.

I open my eyes in empty space, leaving the ledge with a push. My breath burns away and I am light, waiting, with no more substance than a leaf at the reach of a spider's thread. In this pause I'm thin and transparent. I could be that leaf. Or a sail, billowing full.

I close my eyes and I find the fall. I hear the rock wall skim past. The rush of the quarry rising. My body tips and lengthens, extending itself into the descent, arms out at first then closing together. A swarm of air and a coolness.

I can feel the still reach of the glassy water rushing toward me. I know if I open my eyes I could watch my body plummeting toward itself, tumbling loose from the blue sky.

Emma's smile breaks wide. "What are you laughing at?" she asks, her voice hoarse with exhaustion, her smile curling to one side in a private, intimate gesture. And I smile too, not knowing what to tell her, not realizing I'd been laughing.

The water bursts over me with a roar and a sudden hush, blotting away the light. The shock snaps my body into place around me. I'm thrown deep into the lake, momentum pressing hard, the water growing colder in the descent. I open my eyes but see nothing. I tunnel into the dark.

Finally, I drag to a stop, my lungs aching. I hang in the interim just before rising, before the pull of air and the cloudless blue sky draw me back.

I fall again, upward this time. I'm laughing in the fall. Emma hears my laugh, her body sloped into mine, her breathing shallow and quick. She squeezes my hand. She laughs too.

Afterward, I'll try to make sense of it all. From the swim and press and hush. From the flutter of memory and what lingers in my flesh. I'll place everything in a proper order, singular tiles set into a new mosaic. Afterward, it might all become a single story.

Now, everything happens at once. I rise from the dark toward Emma and the blanket. I break the surface with a deep and gasping breath.

THE REASON THE DRESS IS YELLOW

There's a reason the dress is yellow, a reason it glows like a solitary candle in a darkened window, the cloth of the skirt folding in on itself then unfurling in tiny ebbs; there's a reason but if he asks, I won't tell him.

It's possible the dress began something, became the cause of some sequence, the sunburst instant of a new universe or history.

In the dressing room mirror, months before, I hadn't known what the dress was for, what kind of artifact it might become. I'd only known my nakedness before the mirror and the anticipation of my skin just before I slipped it over my head, known that the moment was a threshold between darkened rooms.

A long clench, finally loosening. An ending, for sure, and possibly a beginning.

Like the pop of a sole firefly, rising gently in its own glow, signaling some silent intention against the night.

And when the lemon-colored shoes came later it seemed two clouds were meeting in a vast sky and forming their own weather; combining as a stronger, easier assurance in some direction I couldn't yet discern.

They'd been in the window of a store I'd never noticed on a street I rarely walked down. They'd been waiting for my approaching footsteps. Waiting for my glance.

And when I turn my leg right to left before the mirror, swiveling it in then out on the heel, the shoe seems a perfect extension of the leg emerging from the liquid folds of the dress, the breadth of skin between the bands of color some secret not yet told.

A secret I'd anticipated without knowing, something I'd been waiting for as a turn, a shift. The way despair might be a simple coming to rest. Or the sounding note of a new song.

An ending. As if a book were being closed, ancient blooms and leaves pressed between the pages for so long they've grown ghostly and translucent. The tarnished and brittle back pages of my life.

I'd packed the dress. As if I knew. I'd unpacked it, draping it over the anonymous hotel chair; then, unsatisfied, smoothing it along the blank bed. Sideways, across the bed, hem overhanging at one end, shoulders at the other. It lay there. Waiting for me.

So, I call him.

Out of the blue. Years gone by. Knowing he could have become another person. Knowing he might be anyone now.

I call him and his voice changes shape after the first hello, when I tell him it's me, opening out blooming into the open trumpet of a flower or the reach of a high tree, something solid, regal, and true.

I tell him I'm in town for a conference. And I am.

"Would you like to get together for coffee or something," I ask. The line between us glinting like a thread of web in the sun, glinting for an instant, invisible the next.

He says: "Yes, of course." Though there was no *of*

course to it until the phone call, until our voices wound together like a single climbing vine.

There's a reason the dress is yellow, like the dappled light through the topmost branches of a spreading tree; there's a reason and if he asks me, I might tell him.

I walk to the restaurant. He'd chosen one close to the hotel, not hard to find, with tables on the sidewalk. Thai, because he remembered I like Thai. The sky is open between the buildings, a deep blue with occasional clouds like thin and fine thoughts hardly cohering. The glaze of afternoon light on a wide pane of glass.

I hear my heels on the sidewalk. The steady confidence of my stride. I see the blaze of my reflection pass in a shop window, then another. Something like a melody heard in the distance. Familiar but unnamed.

He doesn't know years of me, the different lives I've had; he doesn't know my other clothes. What he'll see after these years, what he'll know, is the yellow dress that contains me, binds me to earth, pours my legs into the lemon-yellow shoes fastening themselves to the sidewalk.

Yellow is where I choose to stand. The yellow of a saffron robe or a flag whipping in a high breeze. The yellow of mango flesh, still clutching skin, cut away from its fibrous core.

Within the dress I know I am changing. If he asks, I could tell him. Reveal myself beyond my yellow shell. Simple, open, and warm. Flashing bright and sudden like the spark that ignites when I see him again.

Nearly a block away. At a table on the sidewalk in the golden evening light. His legs are canted to the side, his head tilted upward into the clear sky, his hand resting open by his glass. He is waiting. He is patient. It seems he could wait all evening.

I am done with waiting. I have cocooned long enough. Later, should the dress fall away, it will reveal new skin. Fresh, wet; green as a tight bud.

He could be anyone. So could I.

CLOUD CHAPEL

Memory is prayer or possession," she'd told me once, "which do you want?" She hadn't known what she meant and, even when I asked her later, she couldn't explain it. Her expression was strangely confused then, as if I might be mistaking her for another person, a person dimly remembered from long ago.

And when she actually is a person remembered from long ago—eight or nine years later—I still recall her comment, more of a declaration really, in the midst of a now-forgotten conversation.

"I don't know what I mean," she'd told me. "Do I have to know what I mean?" She tugged at my sleeve across the table then slid her palm up my forearm, thrumming her fingers at my elbow. "I just say things. I figure out what I'm talking about later." She was teasing me. "Life's more interesting that way, don't you think?"

The moments of quiet come tumbling back, the moments when nothing was happening. As if our life together had been composed of pauses and transitions, the eccentric architecture of alleyways and doorsteps.

What returns are the spaces between, when we were simply together, not the things that actually occurred. Whatever they were.

As if our hush had placed the cornerstone of a structure in some inner landscape, its shape coming together shadow by shadow, each moment of quiet adding more detail. And later, when we no longer knew each other, there were moments of stillness with others that built upon that foundation. A door, a vaulted window, the suggestion of a roof.

It's a structure I can occasionally enter at will. At other times, I find myself spirited away all at once. Blinking, disoriented, yet somehow calmed. It's a shelter, this still place.

Sometimes in that stillness, she will be with me: her smile, her touch, or the timbre of her silence, pulsing like the vanishing tone of a bell. Or, sometimes I discover someone else. Always feeling that, perhaps at the same moment, this remembered person might be pausing somewhere, on a subway platform, by their desk, or at their kitchen sink; and that they might be remembering, not me, necessarily, but a certain bracing quality of silence.

Long after I'd forgotten the full story of our relationship, the individual events linking in a chain, her presence would appear and bloom within me. There was no predicting it; no apparent reason for her sudden arrival. But she would breathe and burn, for a moment or an hour; then her touch would slowly drain away, leaving me with the kind of vital, echoing silence that signified an ending, a beginning.

When she actually re-appears—is it ten years later?—she is a different person and so am I. The touch and presence is no less real. One of our essential lives reaching out toward another.

She calls me out of the blue. Eight o'clock one evening. "Bill! God, I know it's been forever! It's Trish. . ." She's going to be in town next week for a conference. Just a few days. "So, you wanna get together, have coffee or dinner? Talk about the wonders of our lives?"

I meet her downtown. Walking distance from her hotel so she doesn't have to drive. The city has changed a lot in ten years. I meet her at a Thai restaurant because she always liked Thai and they have tables on the sidewalk and it's early May, so the evening light is beautiful and not too warm. I find a table and wait.

The light shifts around me, the angled sun through nearby branches, reflections thrown from the slow stream of cars, the shadows of passersby. There's a constant flicker on my skin. I try not to think forward, to anticipate: to imagine how she has changed, what her life has been.

On the phone, during our brief conversation, she'd still seemed passionate and clear, her words spilling in all directions—an attempt to say everything at once, to brush past words. I'd smiled to myself, perhaps even chuckled, at her voice and the renewed assurance of her. I'd held the phone to my ear, allowing her voice to pour into me.

I sip the wine patiently; it's cold, crisp as a spring apple. I like the damp chill of the glass along my palm, the sharp clink as I return it to the metal table. The sidewalk and restaurants are starting to fill. I return my hands to my lap, allowing them to lie open, easing myself away from scenarios and scripts.

I summon this place of quiet; it opens itself to me, this location I sometimes share. I feel a coolness and the sense of vast space I notice when noise falls away into open air, unable to impress itself.

I have a few pictures, saved from years ago. I'd pulled them from the closet after the phone call. It was a strange ritual I didn't quite understand. I'd spread them on the kitchen table, my fingers stroking the edges of the stiff paper as if their solidity might prove something I couldn't grasp otherwise. I shuffled through them more than once, withdrawing five or six from the stack and laying them side by side, searching for a narrative.

But the pictures didn't connect me to any memory. I could recall the moments they were taken, the beach trip, the picnic, and the hike on the Appalachian Trail, but they had no weight, leading only to more pictures playing out in my head, scenes from a film damaged by time. They might have been a version of us, our life. They might have been someone else.

I find a place for my body in the chair, for my hands in my lap. I find a place for myself on the sidewalk. I find a place for my breath within my body.

"I want this moment to last forever," she'd told me, fingers lacing into mine. I don't know where we were or when. The world around us didn't exist then. We had our own time.

I know the dense spark in her eye, the pressure of her fingers between mine, the way her lip curls into the hint of a smile, the ministry of her touch. "I want to keep saying 'now' and 'now' and 'now.' Just so we never forget."

It's not a picture, this memory. Not a scene from the dimmed film. It's her breath close to me, her palm on my arm, as real as the coolness passing to my fingers from the glass in my hand.

And the stillness is present; it's a music or the soft brush of a voice. The stillness enters me as I enter it and I imagine that, for an instant as she walks from her hotel to the restaurant, the light changes around her; for an instant, the stillness overtakes her.

It isn't sharp or demanding, it's not enough to break her stride. Only enough that she might smile to herself or notice the open sky; her eyes rising to the break between buildings, the deep blue and the high, voluminous clouds shifting in their passage.

What I learned from her, then, was that every truth is one part mystery. That the shadows between things might be things themselves. She taught me wonder: her eyes flaring at the glimpse of a firefly, her hand dipping into a cool stream, her body swaying in a certain rhythm, her lips parting for a kiss.

"You make me crazy!" I told her, more than once. And her smile in response always filled me with joy. We might be standing on a hillside in the darkness, staring into the night sky, her arm outstretched, her hand open and moving against the night as if nudging the stars into alignment. I would offer my exclamation and she would smile, bumping against me, the heat of her body at my thigh, my arm.

And maybe that never happened, or perhaps I've blended events to shape my experience; or maybe I've simply invented a gesture that feels clear and true and made it real to myself.

"I knew it would be alright to call," she'd told me on the phone. "Even though it's been so long. I knew you wouldn't mind. I knew you would always be you."

There's the hush of her, silent in the next room, sleeping perhaps, as I read by the window or wash the last dish. The hush of her in the apartment, something light and full, reminding me of morning. There's her presence in the corners, in the creases of the furniture, like the damp scent of sex on a pillow.

There's nothing to hold these memories, they're smooth and formless, never still, as fluid as the shadows on the tabletop. They flicker and drop, leaving a darkness that is a waiting or a glorious pause in the breath.

We're driving and she's slumped in the passenger seat, her legs up, bare feet on the dashboard, toes wiggling in time to the radio. The windows are open and the air whips by me in a roar. Strands of hair blow across her face and she doesn't brush them away. Eyes closed, fingers tapping a rhythm on her thigh. She's forgotten me for a moment, and that's okay: I can watch her, my eyes moving from the road to her and back again.

I look up and she is there. Watching me. Motionless, half a block away. People streaming past on both sides.

She's older. Her hair is longer and pulled away from her face. Her dress is yellow. Her skin tanned. A smile curls at one corner of her mouth, her eyes claiming the part of me that knows her.

Words have slipped away. There is sound disguised as motion; noiseless; the rush of something opening in the air. Silent bells at fever peal.

"Well, look at you," she says, not yet moving toward me.

I find a place for my body in the chair, for my hands in my lap. I find a place for my breath within my body. I stand to meet her, hands outstretched. I find a place for her in my life.

If only for a moment.

OPENING

The music is a fog between us, warm and ripe, intimate as skin. It's a heat generating our limbs bone to bone. Nathan's guitar bobs hip to opposite thigh, his right foot rising to the toe then dropping on the downbeat. My eyes are closed most of the time, but I know we're facing each other, facing the roar between his guitar and my voice.

The crowd is churning; they'd been completely his for the last three songs, before he called me to the stage. The entire night has been one gradual ascending climb and now we've collected at the summit, appreciating the arrival as much as the destination.

There's the blaze of the audience, their sway, and the collective stamp at every fourth beat; the subtext of their voices as they hum the melody or sing along, all a vibrant foundation for my own reach. I can feel Nathan's band shifting around us, feel them pass close.

I blink, catching sight of the cloud of Nathan's hair swarming over his fingerboard, Mark's fists coming down hard on the drums. Red lights, blue shadows, a band like a single elegant thought, like a family. I close my eyes again and my voice opens to the room until it takes its own light and weight. The other voices rise around mine, the crowd a few steps away and Nathan's close at my ear, deep and rough, a jagged rasp that somehow softens once it leaves his throat, becoming more rounded and mellow.

My body sways as I sing, my bare arm brushing his. The air shifting in waves of cool and warm, the dance of the guitar and the thump of his foot on the floor. My arms are marking their own language into the air. There's a vast and unknowable space opening around us in the vicinity of dream.

And we are burning, some flame enveloping us. His body so close, the song driving us forward, our arms slick with sweat, glancing, sliding off one another. I have one hand on the mic stand, using it as an anchor as I tilt toward Nathan and the raw edge of his guitar. I lean into him, our shoulders grazing, the heat damp now, damp with our bodies in the glare of the lights and the burst of the music.

I let go of the mic stand and rest my fingers on his shoulder. His body so close as we enter the last chorus and, because it bursts into a ragged and full blaze, we do it again, not yet wanting this song to end or the frame of this horizon to disappear. The room loses its shape, threatening to vanish forever.

We do it again and with the last note we stand, feet apart. His body so close, we declare a silence as if all music were a strategy for arriving at silence. We hold ourselves in the stillness for an instant. I open my eyes and Nathan leans into me, his lips against mine, and his arms enfold me, the guitar between. He lifts me from the floor and we spin, one, two, three turns, in the final peal of our stillness, then into the leap and shout of the crowd.

I'd been lucky to get the job. It was a club we'd never played before, larger than we'd played before. Over our heads, really. Maybe I simply walked in at the right moment or maybe the previously booked band had just died in a fiery plane crash; whatever it was, the owner looked relieved as he quizzed me on my music and the places we'd played. Never even listening to the demo, he offered me a gig only two weeks away.

"You heard of Nathan Driscol?"

"Sure, he's. . ."

"You'll be opening for him."

My eyes widened, my mouth fell ajar. I tumbled into thoughts of what songs we could possibly do with Nathan Driscol in the building.

I reached out to shake his hand. "Deal."

The next thing to do was to get a band together. It wasn't that I didn't have a band, it was just that I didn't have a band. I had Edgar on drums and we wrote songs, or I wrote songs, picking them out on guitar for him, then working them out between us. Later, he'd find a guitarist, a bass player, now and then a violin or an accordion, and now and then they'd play three or four gigs with us before drifting off into drunken binges or construction jobs.

Keeping a band together for more than two months was as improbable as capturing clouds. Unless I wanted to sleep with them, buy their drugs, or bail them out of jail. Which I didn't. So they stumbled through like vagrants at a bus station, always en route to somewhere else.

Edgar isn't impressed by the possibility of opening for Nathan Driscol, leaning more toward Scandinavian Metal as he does, but he is impressed by the venue.

"It'd be cool to play a place that big. Must hold four hundred or so." He's stroking his bushy, unkempt beard, "I bet I can get hold of Tom and Sylvan."

"I'll get back to you," he mumbles, shambling toward the rear of the store. I'm trapped at the register and can't follow to ask what instruments Tom and Sylvan might play.

I can talk about music with Edgar. Mostly he nods or, occasionally, grunts equivocal agreement, in the way one might humor a younger sister. I'd been back at Marino's Books for three months before we ever made eye contact.

It was a slow process, warming up; but now, twice a week or so, whenever we work together, we eat our lunch under a tree in the median of the parking lot and talk music. I talk and he listens, politely engaged, or he becomes excited about some new Norwegian Math Metal band with an unpronounceable name, and I relish watching his eyes light up and his body jitter.

But he is who I have to talk to. No one in my family cares much about music. They don't notice it. They don't notice anything, actually. It's something I never understood. Something I find constantly mystifying.

I could never learn to be blank and incurious before the rumble of the world, could never see it as closed and cold; as if it isn't constantly calling for embrace, as if it isn't always whispering, humming, shouting, luring me into its sink and swim.

So, I grew up awkward in my skin, nurturing secrets, clutching all passions close; an agent behind enemy lines always concealing my true identity, constantly on guard against the revealing mistake.

I wrote songs in a notebook I hid under my mattress. I hid it, not because my mother might be horrified should she find it, but because it wouldn't matter to her one way or another. And that horrified me.

As soon as I could drive, I traveled to nearby towns for open mics. I was awful, screeching my teenage passion into my shoes while clawing at my guitar. I wanted to sound like Fiona Apple or PJ Harvey or Ani di Franco. I thought I had something to say, I thought I had to have something to say.

I never saw the audience when I sang, hunched over the fingerboard, hair shielding my face. I never talked to anyone. I sang my song and ran. I didn't want them to hate it before I liked it; I didn't want them to like it before I liked it.

I was struggling to find something in memory that had never actually happened, yet nagged nonetheless. I just wanted to hear myself in a voice I recognized.

After a few months, the regulars would nod or smile when I entered the room. They'd attempt pleasant conversation. But I didn't know the language. I had no voice. I was comforted by the assurance that, unless I came back the next month, I never had to see them again.

Until I did. Until the day Marietta walked into the bookstore. Her face lit up and she rushed toward me at the register.

"You're that girl," she said breathlessly, "always comes to the Abingdon Open Mic and runs out the door after. I don't even know your name."

I shuffled the books before me, flustered and stuttering. "I'm . . . Sarah."

Marietta was tall and broad with flowing gray hair, partial to blowzy flowered skirts and sandals. She had a deep, full voice she seemed to dredge from far underground when she sang, her body rolling between notes like a boat in a swell. I enjoyed her spirituals most, but now and then she'd sing a dirty blues number and I'd find myself laughing along with everyone else.

"Sarah!" She extended her hand and I was forced to take it. "Marietta."

She held my hand and patted the top with her other. I wanted to sink beneath the counter, terrified my co-workers had now been ushered into my secret life. I stared at our hands, clasped together, hers older, broader, fingertips calloused from years of playing.

She looked into my eyes, but I avoided hers. Finally, she released me, her palms sliding away and folding together, prayer-like before her.

"You keep singin', girl," she told me, her inflection making it seem a command. "It's what you do."

It took three months to work up the nerve to go back to the Abingdon Open Mic, but when I did, I spoke to Marietta. Each time after, she'd greet me with a hug and we'd talk a bit. Sometimes about music or my singing, sometimes not. She was always engaged and immovable, rooted somehow, like a tree dancing in a breeze.

She'd tell me about my breathing, where I'd taken a breath and where I should have, or make cryptic suggestions, asserting a song needed a little more red in it. One night she clutched my forearm and drew me in close.

"You know, we all gonna be judged by how often we escape time." She winked, knowing I had no clue what she was talking about.

I went away to school for a year. When I decided that was a bad choice and came home, Marietta had moved. No one was exactly sure to where.

So, I make do with Edgar, and he manages to put up with me always suggesting rehearsals and new gigs and open mics and playing in empty fields if the cows don't mind, trying to make something happen with a band as impermanent as weather.

Edgar's in front of me, pulling on his beard the way he does when he's annoyed or interested. "Yeah, they can do it. Tom and Sylvan. That's a bass and a lead."

"When can we get together?"

"You mean, before?"

"Yeah, we've got to rehearse."

Edgar sighs. "Aw, Sarah, they know what they're doing, they can. . ." I stare him down. He shrugs, still tugging at his beard. "Alright," he mutters, "I'll call 'em back."

I'm the one who gets the gigs, sets up the rehearsals, puts up the posters, creates the Facebook event pages. I'm the one attempting to coax people into our empty web. I'm the one who shows up an hour early to the venue, because I'm anxious that way, believing somehow if I demonstrate great restraint and responsibility, the guys will at least be there on time and ready to play.

And this time it works. Tom and Sylvan had been good about our two rehearsals, arriving on time and

huddling together to work out their parts. They'd
seemed to like the songs; a nod between them, a smile
to me. Shoved in a corner of Edgar's parents' basement
between the lawn mower and croquet set, we'd worked
through six; the ones Edgar thought best.

I was grasping into darkness, using the rhythm
they laid down, the gentle weave of Sylvan's guitar, for
leverage; clutching it and swinging out into the dark,
all the time searching for purchase, something I could
use to pull myself into the song. All the while feeling
dishonest with the band. As if I should already know
these things.

But the guys liked it. They told me I sounded great
and seemed excited about the gig, the possibility of
playing together again. Still, I sigh with relief when
their station wagon pulls up to the stage door and all
three climb out. Habit, I guess. We stack the gear by the
door, getting it all in before deciding how to set up in
the cramped space the roadie has left us at the front of
the stage.

When they kick into "Steamroller" it's a shock somehow, as dark and charged as walking into a thunder-
head. I close myself around the mic stand, head down,
lips to metal, something dangerous rising in me. The
crowd is loose; it always is at shows like this. There are
loud conversations by the bar, a couple making out at
one table, a few curious onlookers drifting toward the
front of the stage. I'd scanned the room before we started; I know what's out there.

But damn the guys sound good and the song lights
up something in me.

"You always get feisty with that one," Edgar had
observed with a low chuckle. "It'll be a good place to start."

There are random claps after the song, a wolf whistle
from the bar. Bottles clank, a burst of laughter from
the corner. I turn to Edgar, who's tightening a drum; he
glances up, grinning. By "Chupacabra," I'm finding a
place to stand, feet apart, both hands at the mic, leaning

forward and back into it, hitting a certain growl in the chorus I'd always heard but could never reach.

I arch back into the last note of the second verse and when I come up level again, I'm staring out across the floor. There are fifteen or twenty in front of me, twenty or so more toward the back of the bar. People would start arriving now for Nathan. They don't care about us.

But, there's a woman off to the left. Straight, dark hair; simple t-shirt and jeans. She's a few years older than me, with a guy who keeps glancing back to the bar where all the fun seems to be. Eyes closed she sways, bottle between two fingers at her hip, her body lost somewhere in our sound and when I push my way into the chorus as hard as I can, she flushes, a heat rising in her face. Her head slips back into her sway, shoulders rocking as she swings right to left.

I watch her, wanting to wrap the song gently around her. I'm planted and clear, some part of me seating itself in my joints, arms rising before my chest as I throw my head back into the last run of the chorus.

Her loose hand reaches out blindly for her boyfriend's and he turns toward her, then curiously to me, where his gaze lingers for a moment before drifting off, her sway communicating up his arm even as he turns away.

I mutter something once the song ends. I kneel down for my water bottle and notice Nathan, angled into a doorway at the side of the stage, arms crossed loosely over his chest.

We'd met earlier, a kind of guttural acknowledgment of mutual existence passing between us while Edgar talked to the roadie. Nathan is a few years older, tall and lanky, his hair a wild dark thought. He shrugged in conversation as if suspicious of language.

"Hi, I'm Sarah," I extended my hand, "So happy to meet you, to be opening. . ."

His fingers were long, his grip firm but momentary. "Hi, Sarah. Nathan." And then he was gone.

Edgar counts off for "Inside/Outside" and I follow him, trying to ignore Nathan slouched in the doorway, swinging my vision into the room where a few more have stepped forward. I vow to make it impossible for anyone at the bar to have a conversation, finding new places for my voice to birth itself, my eyes coming back now and again to the woman on the left, who rises with each verse and centers down into the choruses.

At the last song, I'm lost and empty, hollowed to something thin and sharp. With the final note, the woman opens her eyes; hers meet mine and she smiles. I say thank you for the group, stepping away from the mic. On the steps of the stage, Nathan touches my arm.

"Nice set," he tells me, eyes clear as if I've suddenly taken form.

"Thanks."

He leans in closer. "You need to get a real band," he confides.

"Well, I. . ."

He taps my arm with his forefinger. "Listen, I oughta get up there," he points toward the stage where everyone is shifting monitors and amps.

"Listen," he taps, "Stay close."

So, I lean in the doorway, taking his position, watching as they run through equipment checks, kick cables out of the way, set mic levels. Edgar and the guys are at the bar by now, having shoved all our gear into the station wagon. I lean in the doorway, wondering what Nathan had meant. By anything he'd said.

They begin slowly, quietly, Nathan growling a hello into the microphone, the crowd shouting back. The room has filled by now but there's still traffic at the bar and in the shadowy outskirts of the club. The crowd jostles itself, stretching and yawning, making itself comfortable.

They begin slowly, quietly, as if they're marking time while everyone finds their place. Then, they burst into a white heat and never stop burning. Nathan pulls the crowd away from the bar, from each other's arms, from the corners and the darkness. He pulls them into a singular body before him. The bar isn't doing any business at all.

I watch as they roar and buck, settling to a low purr and whine for one song, then winding back into full assault for another. The band allows no empty space, no silence, no noodling or tuning; always a low drone or a beat, always a full extended note leading into the next song.

The room warms from the press of the crowd and the music burning off their skin. Nathan's body hunches then explodes, clenching and opening like a fist. He pushes toward them, punching his voice into the thick of them, leaning out from the stage, or settling into place still and simple, repeating the gesture one song after another, each time a little further out and a little further back. Inviting them. Drawing them with him.

The crowd is churning; they've been completely his for the last three songs, when he turns toward me, extending a hand. "I want to bring somebody up here. I was watching her from the back. Can't leave town without doing a song with her." It's two sentences more than he's spoken to the crowd all night.

He's leaning into his guitar player, their heads tilted low, cupped hand to ear. The crowd is cheering, clapping above their heads. I'm scorched and tremulous. I pull myself from the doorway and toward him.

The guitar player nods as I cross the stage, moving a few steps from center toward the drummer, shouting something I can't hear above the noise. There's a low roaring drone, an insect hiss, all around us.

The stage is an oven. Heat bakes off the bodies and bounces from the floor. Nathan is blanketed in sweat, his shirt gummed to his back and arms, hair dripping.

He leans in, mouth to my ear in the roar. "Do you know 'Salesman'?" I nod, staring at a place on the floor.

"Sing that."

I look up to him. "But it's your song."

"Go ahead," he nods. A slight smile, a soft permission. "We'll follow."

For a moment, I'm sure I don't know the words. Or I'll forget them. My knees quiver and I'm terrified I'll drop to the stage, or my voice will be swallowed by his band, and I'll be left stranded like a baby bird.

An anxiety followed, for an instant, by a reprieve: I'm seven or eight, I'm ten or eleven, I'm lying on my back in a meadow staring into the open sky, my body a simple receiver: the clack and warble of distant birds, a hiss of faraway cars, the low hum of the earth and the roar of my own blood; the planet arranging and revealing itself before my senses. The vast swarm of the world and the shape of noticing, always a different, changing form: a melody or a rhythm, the way two words can click together and glow, a glance across a room. I'm lost in a cloud of new temperatures and seasons.

Then, the guitar kicks into the intro, Nathan shifts away from me toward the crowd and, all at once, I know exactly where I am.

My feet touch ground and Nathan releases me, dizzy from our spin, dizzy from the noise swamping the stillness and the push of the crowd. Losing my place again in my body, in the world, after so long away.

Nathan raises his arm to the room in goodnight. He takes a step back, arm dropping toward me and I step forward. The room is full, the crowd exultant; chanting, applauding. I cannot find the woman I knew from before. I give a slight bow and make my way from the stage. I take my place in the open doorway, trying to find breath, waiting for their next songs.

But Nathan is finished, pulling his guitar over his head and unplugging it from the amp. The rest of the band nurses noise from the crowd, who clap and stamp in reply. Nathan brushes past me across the threshold and I roll along the doorframe into the back room. We're both flushed, breathing hard, fingers twitching, skeeved with adrenaline. My back is to the wall; he paces the room a few steps before returning.

"Well, that was fun," he announces nervously. His

face has lost its stance and distance, his eyes are bright and wide. I feel a new blush rising; I nod, stupidly searching for words. I don't know if he's going to apologize for the kiss or kiss me again but, if he reaches out for me, I know I'll drop into his hand.

Thank God, he doesn't.

Even though, for an instant we are together, a murmuring joy passing between us: a joy of recognition, of remembrance.

His eyes drop to his sneakers, arms collapsing with his gaze, and he tilts side to side, lips working toward the next sentence.

"It was great. Thanks so much," I tell him.

I touch his arm and, instead of opening in a gesture of intimacy, the touch somehow becomes one of closure; the hand pausing on the doorknob or the final bittersweet wave. He doesn't seem to notice.

"Sarah, it's Sarah, right?"

I nod. He's innocent and boyish, awkwardly stumbling over his words. "Listen, let me get an email or a Facebook from you. I mean, we're on the road for a few months now. But I'd love to hear how you're doing."

Nathan is searching the room for a pen as the band stumbles through the door, falling into each other, the roar and stamp of the crowd following.

"Are we going back out there?" the guitarist asks. "They're making a shitload of noise."

"Just let me. . ." Nathan's found a sharpie. He scrawls my email address onto his forearm, just before the guy tugs him through the door.

There's a smile, just before the door. It's a gift; it lets me know what's real. And then he's gone. I slip out the side door during the encore.

In the car the dark road unrolls beneath the dark sky, one an endless reflection of the other. I don't turn on the radio. I listen to the faint high hiss of the tires on the road, noticing the shifts in pitch as I slow in curves or accelerate when the road opens.

I'm seven or eight, I'm ten or eleven: I'm staring. The sky so close I can taste the willowy clouds, cool and clean, feel them enter my lungs. I'm on my back in a meadow and the clouds are forming their promises. I'm singing. It's a thing my body accomplishes of its own. There are no words, only a thrill in the sound as it shapes itself in my breath and around my tongue, then leaves me.

And I am not alone.

FORENSICS

She comes in a dream. As herself, not as an animal or a witch. She appears sitting quietly, speaking to me calmly, her hands folded in her lap. Saying she is sorry. And I know that she is. In the dream.

So many years ago. So many lives lived in the meantime. So much time to change who we are and leave us the same. She looks the way she did years and years ago, of course. It was a dream.

It's that hungry time of the morning, between three and four, when you realize you won't be sleeping at all and you'll have to be at work soon. She sits on the edge of the thrift-store bed in our two-room apartment and neither of us can be more than nineteen, twenty. Stumbling into some city from somewhere, young enough to believe it could make a difference, that simply living in the city might transform us into adults and fill us with fresh promise.

She's wearing a worn blue chenille bathrobe, cinched at her waist, now gaping open to reveal her pajama shirt and the funnel of open skin beneath her neck. Her hands lie palms up within her lap and she's staring down into them, shoulders slumped. Her eyes are swollen, her cheeks scaled with dried tears.

I'm standing by the dresser, near the door, resting one elbow among the loose change, clock radio and discarded pencils. The room is hot, the air damp, and we've run out of words, hateful or otherwise, for each other. Staring at the floor, the blank wall, the ceiling. Staring at our hands. Shifting uncomfortably in our bones, wanting to be somewhere else, to be with someone else. To be someone else.

Nothing moves in this room. It seems that nothing can move. The furniture, the bodies, the oily light of the bedside lamp are all fixed, entangled one with another. A crime scene photo. Chalk lines on the floor.

I remember the drive there. In the room and in the dream. Everything we owned in the trunk and back seat. Photo albums and a family quilt. CDs and a portable stereo to play them in. Clothes packed in liquor store boxes. We hadn't told her parents or mine, simply loaded everything while they were out of the house and pointed the car in one direction. Away.

Sandy has her seat tilted back and her bare feet on the dash before her, one arm hanging out the window. The other hand taps out the beat of the song on the radio at my bare knee. Her fine brown hair feathers into her face but she doesn't brush it away. Every now and then, she turns in her seat to peer out the back window into the wide ribbon of road folding up behind us.

A week later, we spend ten dollars at the Dollar Mart on framed pictures and figurines to make the apartment ours. We make love on our own bed in our own apartment as if it were a honeymoon.

A year and a half later, a dark river has bubbled up from beneath the earth to rise between us, skewing the pictures on the wall, cracking the floorboards. There, in the room, in the dream, the water roars in my ears. Minutes before, I'd felt I was drowning, sinking below the surface for the final time, hands clutching in a panic for something hard and sure.

I was struggling with a formless weight which had settled at my chest, the blind hysteria of breathlessness, spinning out, flailing, as if everything could be solved by shifting my position within the room. Too frightened to recognize the lifeline or grasp the outstretched hand. I am catching my breath now, leaning upon the dresser, my teeth clenched, jaw set.

Sandy brushes a nonexistent wisp of hair away from her eyes and allows her hand to drop again into her lap. I feel her breath shallow, learning her body her taste and the delicate construction of her thought over the last two years. I feel her shoulders sag. I know the scent at the base of her neck and the delicate resolve of her chest, having rested my head within the curve. I know the slight tension which sparks along her collarbone just before she speaks. I feel the lump in her throat, in the room. In the dream.

We are trapped in the room where we built and lost our secrets, both the construction and the surrender equally mysterious and unfathomable. Surrounded by the objects which described our twenty-year lives, the only years that really mattered spent together. We are captured in the photo just before, or just after, the earthquake, the explosion, the ravaging fire.

She looks up to me. In the dream. She is no longer sobbing, her tears simply pooling in her eyes. Her lips no longer tremble; her lips are slightly parted, full and red. Her right eye is swollen, a large bruise darkening around it and a thin crescent below. She looks up at me with a question she will not ask and I cannot answer.

We were young, too young. In the room and in the dream. She was telling me how sorry she was, and I believed her and that made everything worse.

KNIFE

Flesh parts. My flesh parts. I spread my legs, opening myself. You see that as an invitation. But there is something required first. Something necessary. You don't ask. You don't want to know. You want it to remain silent. Unspoken. You're already forming an apology for later.

I am not waiting for you. My body flutters like a petal upon a single stem. It rises and falls within its own currents. It does not need a whisper from you. I keep my own secrets. Folding them within me, pressing them into the creases, the soft openings in my flesh. I hold them on my tongue, on the tips of my fingers, between my legs. My secrets are encoded in my body where no one can read them until my flesh parts. I don't have to worry about you.

You stand watching, your subtle smile, the heat along your chest. You breathe as if you know but my language is closed to you. It's an exotic dialect you can't perceive as language.

I bend my knee, fingers along the threads of my inner thigh, a fine wheel turning high within me. And you,

you don't want to speak. Your every muscle straddles bone and aches for a tension as clear as the flat of my hand at your cheek.

So, you ask me out. Bring me here, to this restaurant. Sit across the table from me over hot and sour soup and search for a way in. Your words probing, your eyes hot.

You want to leap to the last dance. Scheme it all out after, tease the knowledge from the memory of my flesh. First, you want to fall far into forgetting. Dragging yourself onto the beach later, certain that now you are a hero and a castaway.

But I won't let that happen. I won't let you sink below the white water. I'll hold your head above the curling waves by your hair and never allow you a liquid breath. No matter your begging and tears.

Flesh parts. I open myself but will not allow you to drown. I've already heard your apology and I do not forgive you.

I live thirty seconds from a scream.

I've measured it once or twice, the time it takes if I let everything go. The time elapsed before the force of the terror is there, white-hot and barbed, clutching at the pit of my stomach. I relax a little, allow my mind to slacken, but the tension kneads at my shoulders, my hips, seeping toward the center like India ink upon a burgundy cloth.

Before I close everything down. Slam the doors to all the open rooms, ignore the immensity of the house, and collapse into the dark and cool of the closet.

Sometimes, I let it happen. I let the scream come. Let it vomit forth like a foul, dark liquid the color of old blood. Screaming until it tears my throat and cramps my stomach and twists me into a knotted snarl of flesh on the floor.

But all that screaming doesn't help. When I open my eyes I'm still in the closet and the closed rooms still lurk, down hallways behind doors, with an idiot constancy.

The last one called me unstable, but I know more about stability than he'll ever imagine. I know every bolt and nut, every joint and eave. I count, every morning, the number of nails required to compose that structure.

That scream, its roots clotted in my chest and knotting down my legs, always thirty seconds from the light; it's the closest I get. That scream, cutting its way loose from my body, is the closest I get to knowing all I need to know. About me.

The lover is incidental, an arm prone along my abdomen, a foot curled into mine beneath the sheet, a hair falling against my face with the scent of wine and sex and sleep.

Bodies lie. They don't hold together. Disjunctive, they break into parts and hardly slide back again. The fingers upon my skin, the tongue at my neck, the thigh pressed against mine, they're all struggling to will themselves into form. A body which might hold me in strong arms that I do not dissolve.

I know the weight of those fingers but not the muscles which trace back to heart and bone. Except as a force, a violating blade. I know your touch. Even now, so soon. Your touch which will begin so delicate and loving but will file slowly to an edge scratching out a hollow in my chest in which your breath will nest.

I want to slide into a still pool. If only for a moment. Underwater, we might lose our faces, the pressure of the depths drawing our limbs together and holding them fast so I might follow the trace of your touch fully up your arm. Into the sinews of your neck and the shallow of your breath.

We could look up together, our eyes blind except for the sunlight puddling upon the surface high above us. The sun no longer a singular orb but dispersed and rippling.

The lover is incidental. He cannot gather the weight necessary to push me below the surface deep enough that I will never have to breathe again. Where faces disappear. Where fingers penetrate beyond bone, fingers growing stiff from the cold in these depths.

I want to slide into the pool where everything enters, its entrance stitching my limbs within the arms of another. I want to share my origin with another like a twin.

I told her one night. In the kitchen. Stayed behind at the table after she cleared the dishes. Told her while her back was turned and her hands were clattering in the sink. Trying to say it without crying but crying, of course, anyway.

She slipped each dish quietly beside the other into the wooden rack on the counter. I watched the water sheet slowly down the facing one and collect into a bead at the rim. I studied that drop, clear and trembling, willing it to fall. But it never did.

I took a lot of baths then, when I was seven. She had a hard time keeping me out of the tub. I would deposit my Hello Kitty book bag by the front door after school and escape to the bathroom without an afternoon snack. I would run the water hot enough to redden my skin then scrub until the flesh was raw.

She asked me what I'd done to provoke him. I don't remember the word she used but you get the idea. She asked me without ever turning away from the sink. What I'd done. Because women always take responsibility for men. All men. We want to be stable. We do not want a hole in our boat.

It always hurts more, what comes after. It's the shadow that fills your life long after the fist has opened.

So, I scrubbed my abraded skin until scabs formed and she dragged me to the doctor and he never thought to ask my secret.

She would never have allowed him to enter our special world, this world of voiceless and noble suffering, of martyrdom, to which I was now initiated.

More a marker of femininity for her than menarche or the sanctified ease of blood.

He told her to watch me bathe, so she stood in the open doorway every night, eyes steady at my fingers, while my father cluelessly questioned the silent mysteries of women.

I lightened my touch, not wanting her close, not wanting her to wash me with her hard, strident strokes. Still wanting so much for her to lift me dripping and limp from the tub, swaddle me in a clean sheet and sing to me softly.

I watched the plates in the drying rack, so I did not have to stare at her motionless back. Depositing my tears back into my body, one by one like coins to a ceramic bank. I could save them there, watch them accumulate and take on weight.

I needed a scar. I wanted a scar. At thirteen. Now. A scar here on my skin where there can be no argument. A secret marker like a box buried deep underground with only a thin branch to reveal its position.

I had to wait until my mother no longer watched me. I stilled my scrubbing hands, feeling the tension ebb back from my fingers, up my arms, into my shoulders and down my spine until I was hard. Solid as a stone. I was awaiting blood, already enthralled by its scent. Anticipating the warmth, the thin trickle snaking down my thigh, dropping bead by ruby bead into the still water below.

The first time. I held the scissor open upon my leg, a thin silver cosmetic scissor near the hinge of my thigh and I relished the certainty of the metal. Cool, hard, and unrelenting. And when I drew it across my skin, when my flesh parted and blood oozed forth, I was no longer solid. No longer a stone but something softer, more vulnerable, a register of touch.

And that scar was mine. It belonged to me. It was the first stroke of a map of secrets I could carve into my body. Each thin line raising to form a topography. My history, my knowing. My secrets. I could, I did, claim my body for myself.

I touched myself and drew blood. I drew blood and made myself real. I claimed my legs, my arms, my breasts and the damp between my legs, reserving only my face for others. My face as the mask, the shield. To protect me from others, to protect me from her.

And when I was older, thirty-one, and she was dying, I was steady at her bedside. Sometimes at night I would slip my hand beneath the taut blue sheet to the loose flesh of her thigh and I would take her skin between my fingers. Pressing and twisting as hard as I could.

The next day, there would be a massive bruise and I would confront the staff at the nurse's station, threatening retribution, nearly deranged by their blatant maltreatment of my mother.

I spent months feeding her, changing her, washing her clothes at home, and returning them folded to her room. Choosing her meals and spooning them into her weakening mouth. Bringing her the chocolates she liked best. Watching her favorite shows.

As she declined, as she stopped speaking, withdrawing from me and into her body, I continued our conversation, day after day after day. And the night before she died, I pushed my hand beneath her nightgown and pinched the flesh of her abdomen above the saddle of her hips until I drew blood.

I stayed with her that night. I fell asleep with my head on the bed by her hand. When the nurse shook me gently and told me she was dead, I looked up at her with blank, unblinking eyes.

That night, at home, my clothes damp from the day, my eyes swollen, I drew a knife from the drawer and stabbed one palm then another. Holding my hands over the sink. Blood dripping bright and hot onto the dirty dishes. I didn't scream then, I wailed. I wailed, knowing I had vanished, that the only witness to my life was a wound.

◆ ◆ ◆

And now, you. Requesting confidences. Across the table with the ease of a sunrise. The menu spread open, you choose confidently. Your certainty as sharp as a blade held hard to my throat.

As if you stared through me at first sight, knowing I had no-one. Believing I was awaiting your word, your invitation. As if you visioned me huddled by the phone anticipating the ring and the possibility of a beginning.

Your hands are quiet upon the table while I turn like a cyclone. Your eyes are blue and open while I burn in all directions.

You ask questions, assured you want to understand. You don't know the answers you want yet, but you will. Soon your face will shallow and smile when I lie but darken when I venture the truth. I will wriggle under your gaze to color within the narrative lines. You want the voice which speaks from the face; the neatly manicured, well-drawn voice colluding in agreement.

People leave. I know. One scream and they're gone. A single glimpse of a darkness and they recoil. Disappearing, even before they leave the room.

You want a lie but would never admit it. You want golden stories of childhood and a mildly inquisitive interest. You want to share beautifully sculpted secrets, trading them like cherished antique toys.

You turn to me in the grocery store with a sly smile, introducing yourself. And I ache to be the one you might love. You cradle a cabbage like a welcoming Pilgrim and in the sway of your crooked grin I struggle to believe in your grace.

It's a new self which inches toward you. A shadow awaiting feature, as faceless as a stone. Adjusting my posture, my syntax. Shifting to your subtle clues, I find a way to be for you.

I want to vanish at your touch. Sink so far beneath

the surface at your fingers that I discover a new voice, uncover new flesh.

For an instant, in your arms folding within your scent and your weight, I take another shape. Leaving my broken and scarred body behind to find a shadow self, held still and clear. You ask and I might ease a single door open. My body rising in the instant of your touch. Your fingerprints, your word, at my breast. Smoothing the flesh lush over my bones.

And I would love you. In the solitude of our tangled bed, I would take your body into mine. I would take you in the arms made strong by your breath. I would not shy from your desires but embody them, making them whole. I would love you. I would love you.

I would become for you. I inhabit the beautiful machine you desire. I lie still and moan. I move where your hands draw me, to the rhythm you choose. My mind is a fine blanket of open snow awaiting your footprint.

Wanting so much. To believe. That your chains might free me. That their weight might bind me to a warming core. Wanting so much to believe, even as I watch my limbs vanish at their bite. Separating at joints. Rattling loose.

And now, you. Struggling to hold my dissolving form. Calling to me as if you know my true name. Keening in my absence as if I had once been clean before you.

You don't know the emptiness I bring. You don't see the blood beneath my nails. You don't know the ragged stump of my heart. You are blind to the jagged truth of the world.

You. Thinking you want me only because you don't know me. There is no shadow which you caress only the raw teeth of the scream which is my soul.

I step back. Away from you. Watching you search for me with your watering eyes and trembling hand. Aground somewhere between your cock and your heart. My body limp beneath you, humid in your heated breath.

And now, you. Here, when I was alright before. Alright within my world. Without someone saying they want me.

You don't want me. You want a lie. A lie you can believe in. A lie you can fuck.

I remember the night was black and burning with stars. I was five or six and I looked up with sleep-glazed eyes through the back windshield, drifting in and out of dream. Aware of the motion of the car. The nearness and the constancy of the stars. I remember turning my face into the seat, my dream accepting the hum of the road passing beneath me.

And when the car came to rest, when we arrived back home, my father opened the back door and the chill winter air raced over my naked face and hands. His firm arms slid beneath me like deepening roots, lifting me from the seat. And for an instant, half awake, I floated there, midway between the car and his body in the cold, silent night. Only the plane of his arms to support me.

In an instant, he drew me to his chest, my head lolling upon his shoulder, my arms loose down his back. His face rasping against mine, his breath pluming around my head. He carried me wordlessly into the house and up the stairs. He lowered me into my bed and drew the blankets to my chin.

And I was safe in the car. Safe in the bed. Safe in his arms. Yet what I remember most is the moment I hung in the air. Waiting to be drawn toward him.

Maybe I'll tell you that story at the table, over dessert. Offer you the moment. If I allow my hands to rest loosely by the coffee cup, if I take my time in the telling and speak gently, maybe you'll understand something small and fragile within me.

Maybe you'll be nice to me. Turn and smile as we stand by the cash register, sharing a silly joke. Hold the door for me when we leave the restaurant. Open my door first at the car.

Maybe, you'll drive me home and we'll talk easily and perhaps I'll watch your hands on the wheel and the way you glance over to me as you angle the car through the blinking and wet night traffic.

I'll slide down in the seat, stretching languidly, allowing a slight yawn, not of boredom but ease. I'll ask you about the book resting upon your back seat.

You'll park the car in front of my apartment, but I won't make a move to get out. We'll sit there together. In the quiet, in the darkness. Nervous, unsure. But relishing the anticipation. And I won't be anxious.

We'll sit in the car. Together. And I will wait. The water will pool quietly at the bumpers, swirling toward the doors. We'll watch it rise all around us. Perhaps we'll feel the tires lose touch with the ground, the car listing gently in the current. And when the water spills through, around the doors, up from the floor, we'll be shocked at first by its cold and its force.

The car will lift and begin to spin away. The water will be relentless. You'll look over at me. I'll turn away, momentarily shy. The water cold upon my legs, rising to my waist, taking my breath. You'll speak my name. Softly.

I won't say anything. I'll hold my breath, waiting for you.

CURRENCY

I'd said the wrong thing, then Lynn said the wrong thing, and before we knew it flame was curling from the pan on the stove, smoke clinging to the air. She leapt for the lid to smother the fire, turning back to me but I had no words left. I couldn't really remember what the argument was about, I only knew the grip of rage at my throat. I walked away. She called my name as I moved toward the door but didn't follow.

Beads of rain rattled from the frame when I slammed the door, peppering my shoulders, cold on my face. The night was slick and oily, the rain indecisive. The glow from the streetlight had tangled itself in the trees. I stood on the porch, searching my lawn for something familiar.

It felt good to settle into the car and pull the door closed, its distinct click carving out a certain silence in the unnerving rhythm of the night. I didn't put the key in the ignition just yet, wanting to avoid its incessant chime. I folded the keys onto the passenger seat, covering them with my hand.

The bitterness scorched through me. Not her bitterness, or ours; something older, scrubbed and claw-like, twisting down my arms and into my fingers, bringing its own responses from the shadows of a past I could no longer decipher. I pounded the heel of my hand at the steering wheel, once, twice, three times, until the sting became an ache rising into my arm.

I was hollowing to a singular note of emptiness, the plummet after rage and blame as adrenalin pulls away, leaving bruised flesh and raw bone. In the absence of rage there was nothing; nothing but the night around me, the night outside the car, beating its constant pulse. I rubbed my hand absently, the pain somehow soothing.

I didn't want to see the house or the light in its windows, the slant of the sidewalk or the shrubs we'd planted in spring to frame it. My eyes lost focus in a kind of willful night blindness. I didn't want to see the lawn unfolding to the road or her car silent next to mine or the large, plain pumpkin resting by the front door. I wanted to be free of the past, the clutch of it, and its blind recurrence. I didn't want to feel the same feelings, think the same thoughts, contend with the cold darkness which always fell after our arguments.

Lynn's perfume lingered in the car like a rootless memory, and it wasn't simply the perfume itself, but its scent once it had become a part of her, after an hour or so on her skin. There was a slight spice, a certain citrus, and the smell of her hair when she was asleep at two in the morning. Recognizing this didn't make me angry at her ghostly presence. It was more a sadness, an unarticulated loss, and the vague exhaustion one might feel at the thought of having to repeat a long journey.

I heard myself sigh. The sound bored me, the tone and the drama of the exhalation, and every faltering pressure framing it. My hands came to rest on top of the steering wheel, my fingers weighted, then curling slightly.

When they touched the underside something sparked, the tips completing a lost circuit, phantom voltage traveling the length of my spine to release a tiny synaptic warmth. Memory tumbled on sensation, side to side and back, never in a straight line, like a child randomly leaping one stone to another. I sank into it, the muscles of my back releasing into the seat, my heavy body receding, falling away, replaced by something smaller, more contained and ecstatic.

I'm bouncing at the knees, clutching the wheel, raising myself up then letting myself drop. I fall back and lurch forward, anchored by the steering column. I can't be more than five, standing on my uncle's legs before the wheel. His voice is close at my ear. Itchy excitement jangles my arms and legs as I struggle to listen, knowing it's important.

"I'll let you drive, but you gotta pay attention."

I bounce on his thighs, bumping my head gently on the roof of the car, enjoying the muffled sound it makes, the tingle along my skull. He chuckles, releasing the handbrake. My hands lock at the top of the wheel while his hover near my waist, thumb and forefinger notched at the bottom, casually suggesting the direction of the car.

I remember the weight of the machine around me. The way the world opened to our motion, changing shape as we passed. The sunlight flickering along the windshield, the canopy of trees gliding by in reflection: green and yellow, blue, then green again. The sense of momentum, of flying, with my uncle's hands applying just enough pressure that everything felt dangerous, but not too dangerous.

Later that day, or the next day, or another year, I'm in the kitchen with Grammy Jane. She's made a grilled cheese sandwich for me and I'm sitting at her sturdy oak table, straightening the sandwich on the plate after every bite, the buttery crumbs sticking to my fingers and my glass of milk when I replace it by the plate. She's as sturdy as a post, planted at the kitchen sink, peering into the backyard, washing a plate. It's spring I think, because it seems warm, and the windows are cast in green. The light is high—sweeping past Grammy Jane from the back yard, filling the room around us.

She turns to me as if I've called her name. Her light blue eyes are deep-set and clear and she's wiping her hands on her apron. My legs are dangling over the edge of the chair above the floor. I pick up my sandwich for another bite and she says, "You are my darling boy."

Her glow passes through me. I remember kicking my legs out in the chair, rocking back and forth, looking toward her then taking another bite. I come into my body, filling it to bursting, something inside growing large to push against the very boundaries of skin. I kick my legs out, bouncing, and the chair rocks leg to leg on the linoleum floor. I chew my sandwich.

And, one night, not so very long ago: it's two in the morning and Lynn thinks I'm asleep. She turns her body toward me in the bed. I can make out the glow of the clock over her shoulder, the numbers blue-white and persistent, and the nest of her hair tousled by sleep. She rests on one arm, her loose hand pausing at the smoothed sheet an inch from my chest before touching me cautiously. She says, "I love you, Sam Lightner. You are the person I love in this world." Her sleep-stained breath glances my forehead, her warmth soaking me beneath the shell of the blanket. She stares at me for perhaps five minutes, and I don't dare move, then she kisses me lightly on the forehead so as not to wake me and turns away, sinking into sleep.

Grammy Jane tucks me into the spare bed at her house. I stayed for weeks that summer because they said Mother was sick and needed quiet, and Dad was away. Grammy Jane sits on the side of the bed. The room is dark, but the door is open and the hall light is on, so a wedge of light spills by the bedposts, draping her lap. She's told me a story of her childhood, of looking for a missing calf with her father, of holding his hand as they made their way down to the creek and feeling his pulse quicken along her fingertips when they heard the first plaintive bellow of the animal, of the way he tossed the calf around his neck, pinning its legs to both sides of his chest. They walked home like that, she bumping close beside him, he with the calf on his shoulders; the animal quiet now, found. She'd been proud of him, proud of his strength, his intelligence and compassion, and the pride came through in her story about a man I never knew.

After the story she sits silently for a time, remembering him perhaps, holding his presence vital within her. She turns toward me. My eyelids are heavy, my limbs melting into the clothesline smell of her sheets. I'm squirming in the bed, too exhausted to be sleepy, too stubborn to be quiet. Grammy Jane starts to talk again, only it doesn't seem she's talking to me, but to herself, or another figure in the room just beyond my vision. Her voice is low, more of a hum or a song.

She talks about things I don't understand, but it doesn't matter; it's the slow intimacy of the moment that settles over me. Her fingers sweep the hair from my eyes and stroke my forehead; her fingers large and rough with work, smelling of flour and lemon and starch. I curl my body around hers on the bed, nestling into her back, and drift into the seat, behind the wheel, allowing something precious to fade and peering after it into a darkness.

All the time feeling I'm constantly looking in the wrong direction; as if I have a story I'll never understand, apocryphal memories which refuse to cohere into narrative. They chart the features of another kind of history unfolding in the shadows, glimpsed but never clear. And what I remember is what I remember, whether it happened or not.

I turn the key and the headlights click off, leaving me with only the night. I pull them from the ignition and place them on the passenger seat, tenting my hand above them. The car settles itself to rest around me.

Lynn would be standing in the kitchen now, making a cup of tea, and the cat would be curling around her leg as he always did when she came to rest by the stove. She'd be staring off to the left, not quite toward the

window. She'd pull the teapot from the flame just before
it began to whistle, twining her fingers around the cup
as soon as she deposited the teabag. She'd spiral into
the armchair around her cup and the cat would settle
into her lap.

Or, she might be coiled and seething, waiting for the
sound of the turning lock to pounce with a harbored rage.

Or, she'd be propped in bed on four pillows, the
comforter at her waist, book resting on her knees.
Her cup would steam on the bedside table. Her glasses
would be partway down her nose, her hair pulled back
with a clip, two buttons of her pajama shirt unbuttoned,
revealing just enough skin that I might stop when I enter
the room and she might peer over the top of her glasses
in my direction, the slightest smile curling at her lip.

I pull up the pictures as if they are snapshots in an
album, or scenes where I linger just above the room.
They're dream images in which I watch myself. I pull
them up. I let them go.

She died before I could get there. She'd managed
to reach the phone, managed to call 9-1-1 and me, at
home in my pajamas in front of the TV while her car lay
crumpled and upside down in a shallow ravine. She'd
managed to stay alive until the EMT's arrived but, she
died waiting for them to cut the metal skin of the car
away from her.

I stand in the wet, black grass, my slippers soaked, my
raincoat whipping around my pajama pants. The night
shudders pulses of blue and red, strobing the branches of
the trees, the landscape unsure of its shape. The gash in the
bank, the gnarled car. Voices run past in both directions,
shouting, dragging themselves up and down the hill.

I drop to sit in the grass, eyes sliding over the blurred
picture, returning to the car door and her limp hand
then sliding away to the blinking trees and back to the
car door, the EMT leaning in through the shattered
windshield, pushing at the door inside with all his
might, and I only know I'm alive by the weight of my

body on the grass, the pulsing grind of the night around me, the hand of gravity forcing me farther downward, hard and unrelenting.

I have not moved her book from the bedside table. I keep her clothes, folded in the drawers. And now and then, in the morning at breakfast or late at night, I turn the phone in my hand for a moment or two before playing one of the last messages she left me. It's unremarkable. It's the one where she says: "I'll be home in an hour or so. I'll stop and pick up a few things for dinner." It's the one where she adds the casual "love you" in that tone we use when we feel something is commonplace and accepted.

I sit in the car, hands resting at the top of the wheel. I don't want to see the light in the curtained windows, the shrubs along the walk rustling in the breeze. I don't want to look. But I do. I stare through the fogging windshield toward the amber glow hanging in the living room drapes and the porch light Lynn had switched on eight months ago when I stormed from the house. I haven't turned it off.

Now and then, when I climb into the car in the morning, I catch the scent of her, present for only an instant. Then, it's lost.

But it's enough. Enough to winnow some tiny pocket within me which allows breath. Enough to remember the laugh she saved for me, the silken lull just below her armpit, her hand finding mine across a table. Enough to remember the nights I fell asleep wrapped in the language of her body.

I've been driving for hours, going nowhere, passing the same familiar stops and landmarks of our history. The car warm now, comforting now, within the sea of night. I'd like to fold into the seat and sleep.

I close my eyes and Grammy Jane sits in the near dark at the head of my bed, stroking my hair in silence. The weeks at home before, the shouts and broken dishes, slide away. Her silence is a comfort. It contains.

I'd asked about Grandpa, what had happened to Grandpa.

Curled within the cocoon of the sheets, it's hard for me to distinguish the music of her silence from her voice. Suddenly she's purring near me, her words low and calm as honey. She's whispering, as if I might remember some phrase or another thirty-two years later. There's music in her voice and it seems I don't hear words at all but a kind of slow and even exhalation. She'd been talking about Grandpa and now she was talking about something else. She tells me, "Praying is a way of knowing something, I guess. A way of saying something." Her hand, wide and warm, rests on my shoulder, as other hands would. "It's a way of being, when there ain't nothin else."

I get out of the car, closing the door softly behind me as if afraid of awakening someone. It's two in the morning and the neighborhood is still, the houses lined blankly on both sides. The road is black and empty. I take two steps from the car and find it's as far as I can go.

I'm looking up, directly into the giant pool of the sky. It's dark and cold, the kind of cold which slips its own crystal tone into the air. The stars are rippling their pasts in my direction, and somewhere there, far into the darkness above me and nearly unnoticeable, there's a sudden note of stillness. It's a stillness which allows the planet to stop.

Lynn's presence pours into me in a jolt with the chaos of weather. It's a great roar, a thing my body can't contain. She turns to me from the edge of the water, our eyes catch and she smiles. A hint of a smile, a ghost of a smile. Lynn says something to me. It doesn't matter what. I take the form her voice allows.

PLEASE

Alice drifts behind her body. Or above it. She has a little distance. The distance is familiar. She floats. She can almost watch herself. Almost. She can almost see herself.

She's old. She knows she is old. She feels age in her knees, her hips. In the looseness of the skin at her arms. She knows she's old by the way she grips the banister on the way down the stairs. To steady herself.

The wide staircase. The carpet under her bare feet. The pictures on the wall. Photos. Young children clutched together. Grandparents around a dinner table. Families. New families, or old ones, families with curious eyes. Some she can recognize while others seem too young, the memory too distant in her blood.

She feels a pulse of lightness. Descending the stairs. Her joints resist. There is a coolness. She can see her hand. On the banister. Her hand is old. The skin is thin and spotted. Her fingers are tightly closed. They slide along the rail. The families watch. They have their own lives, their own voices.

She is empty. On the stairs. She is cold. She wishes

someone were beside her. She imagines a hand, a voice.
Something warm.

Once at the bottom of the stairs, she can see into
the kitchen. Momma would be there. She'll be cooking
dinner.

Lindy says: "G-ma, what are you doing?"

Fifteen. Eighteen. How old is Lindy now. She's tall
and thin and pretty. With wavy brown hair. Soft, bright
eyes. And a confidence Alice never knew. She thinks of
Steph at that age. Of Steph when Lindy was born.

Hair glued to her head with sweat. The nurse
bundling Lindy and lowering her into Steph's arms.
Steph reaching up for her. The way Steph drew Lindy
close and smiled. The smile as she held Lindy for the
first time. Exhausted. Happy.

Alice is looking past Lindy. She can feel herself
looking past her toward the kitchen.

Coming down the steps isn't easy. She could have
stayed in her room. She could have told no one. Coming
down the steps is the most she can do.

"G-ma. You're not dressed. You don't have your pants."

Alice touches Lindy's arm, then her shoulder. She
wants to know that she's okay. She wants to know she
is safe. Instead, she looks past her toward the kitchen.
Momma, she hears herself say. Momma.

"G-ma, we need to get you back upstairs. You need
to get some clothes on."

Lindy is trying to understand. She's being
understanding. Alice hopes Lindy doesn't understand.

Lindy turns Alice gently back toward the stairs.

"I'm gonna call Mom and see when she's coming
home. Why don't you go upstairs and get dressed. I'll
make you some tea."

The stairway is long and narrow. The walls are white
and bare. Damp, because the house is surrounded by
tall spreading trees and always shaded. The stairs are
polished pine. Cold at her feet. She doesn't want to go
back upstairs.

Lindy says: "If you need help, I'll be up in just a minute. Okay?"

Where else can she go.

She is young. She is scared. She puts a foot on the bottom step. She holds on to the banister. She pulls herself up one step. She thinks she is crying. She's crying softly. So no one will notice. She wipes the tears with her free hand.

The landing above her seems so far away. There is weight. So much weight. In her feet. Her legs. She thinks she stops halfway up. She'll turn and sit on the step. But there's blood on her leg. Running down her leg. If she makes a mess, Momma will yell. She'll just stand still for a moment.

Momma, I'm bleeding, she told her. Momma was standing at the stove, still dressed from work. She looked pretty. Her hair still pretty. Her light blue dress. She was stirring something. Daddy was mowing the yard. She could hear the mower pass close by the window. A vibrating growl. The crunch of a twig or branch chewed in the blades.

Momma. Momma turned toward her. Her face hard, her blue eyes cold and sharp. "What are you doing down here with no pants. You get back upstairs. You get dressed. You're too old to be running around like that."

Momma, I'm bleeding, she told her. It was wet and warm down there. It was trickling down her leg. She had blood on her fingers.

She stood at the bottom of the stairs. She didn't walk toward Momma. She blinked. Trying not to cry. The mower passed by the window. It roared and the window-glass rattled.

"That's what women do," Momma said, "we bleed." She turned back to the stove. That's all she'd say about it.

She doesn't look at Alice again. She stirs the pot on the stove. She turns away from her to pick up a knife. She brushes a strand of hair from her face. She's wearing the apron Daddy had given her. It's blue with white stripes.

Alice is frozen at the bottom of the stairs. Her legs won't move. Her feet too heavy. Her hands hang at her side. She can feel their weight. If she stares at Momma too long, she'll yell. Alice stares at the floor instead of Momma.

She tells Alice to get a sanitary pad from the bathroom. She tells her to put her clothes on. She tells her to go upstairs. She doesn't look at her.

"Dinner will be ready soon," she says.

Alice has stopped on the stairs. She's halfway up. She holds to the banister. She's old. She knows she's old because her body is heavy. Her brain is weighted in her skull. She doesn't want to think. She doesn't want to speak. She wants someone to hold her.

She knows her Momma and Daddy loved her. She knows they are dead now. Dead for years. Dead and gone. She wants to love them. She doesn't want to think of them that way. She wants to love them. She does love them. She loves them. They're dead.

Momma was so pretty. And Daddy so handsome. When they were dressed to go out. When she stood on the step with the babysitter to wave goodbye. And when they turned toward the house as the car pulled from the driveway, Alice would talk to the babysitter about everything, and they would play games and draw pictures. Later the babysitter would sit on the side of the bed and tell her a story. And Alice would talk until she fell asleep.

She could talk to them. But they didn't answer. She could tell them she loved them. But they didn't answer. They were dead now.

She doesn't remember what she said. They'd both been drinking before dinner. She was nine or ten and she doesn't remember what she said that caused Momma to punch her. She is sitting beside her at the table and she says whatever she says. Momma turns and knocks her

out of her chair. She hits her head on the wall. She lies
on the floor by her chair.

She doesn't speak during dinner. After that. She's
lost something. She doesn't know what she's lost but
she knows she's lost it. It isn't like losing something she
already had. It's losing something she might have had.

What she lost then. After that, she went to her room
after dinner. She went to her room in the evening. After
dinner. She read and did her homework and drew in her
notebook. She stayed away from them in the evenings.
Especially then. When they were drinking. When they
were loud and broke things. Especially then. What she
lost then, she doesn't know what she lost then.

She's turned on the stairs. She's staring at the landing
below. She doesn't want to go back to her room.
Something isn't finished. She looks down the stairs. From
the bottom of the stairs she could see into the kitchen.

She should call Steph to see if she's okay. To make
sure she's safe. Someone needs to look after her. She
should call Steph. To be sure.

The stairs are unpainted. Raw wood leading to the
concrete floor of the basement and the finished room Joe
had built. It's late. Or very early in the morning. She can
hear the giggles of Steph's middle school friends. Hear
their conversation though she can't make out the words.

She and Joe had gone to bed late. They'd made
popcorn for the girls, brought down sodas. They'd had
a few beers when the girls settled in. Fooled around
a little on the living room couch before going to the
bedroom.

Her hand is on the banister. She just wants to check
on them. Make sure the girls are okay. She's outside her
body. She is above, or drifting just behind. It's always
like that after sex. During. She watches herself descend
the stairs. She calls Steph's name.

It's only later Steph tells her she was naked and all
the girls saw. No pants, descending the stairs, lipstick
smeared. It's only later—the next morning—after the

mothers have come for their daughters, that Steph will talk to her at all and then she's seething. A pure adolescent rage that spins to tears. She slams the door to her room.

"I had to make you go back upstairs. And all the girls were watching. And you were just standing there like nothing was wrong. And all I could say was, Momma go upstairs and get dressed and you wouldn't."

She needs to check on Steph. To make sure she's alright. To know she's safe. That's all she ever thinks about. Steph doesn't realize how much she worries. Steph just wants to talk about the past. She doesn't want to forget. She can't forgive.

Lindy is there now. She's at the bottom of the stairs. From the bottom of the stairs Alice could see the kitchen. Her Momma at the stove. Her Momma who looked so pretty when she left for work, when she came home from work. Her hair all permed and sprayed. Her bracelets. Her perfume. Light and flowery. Like the memory of a flower.

She'd be standing at the stove and Alice could tell her.

"I called Mom, G-Ma. She'll be home in just a bit. She said if you get dressed maybe you guys could go out to the park. That would be nice, right? Get out of the house, into the sunshine? Go on up and I'll be there in a minute."

Lindy is sweet. She's a sweet girl. Lindy is trying to understand.

Alice turns on the stairs to go back up. It's a wide staircase with a smooth, polished banister. The carpet is cool beneath her bare feet. The families, parents, children, and friends peer out curiously from the photos. She wishes she were small, wishes they couldn't see her. But they can. They can see her.

The woman in the next car can see her. The woman at the stoplight in the next car. She doesn't notice at first but when Alice hits Steph the second time and Steph curls into the floor of the car and Alice flails at her, trying to reach her without taking her hand off the steering wheel, pounding at her then clutching her hair and tugging at her head, and Steph is crying now, wailing now, making herself small, Alice looks up all at once and sees the lady in the next car staring at her, her eyes wide, her mouth ajar, and then the light changes and Alice has to let go, has to jerk Steph's head one last time and accelerate through the light, leaving the staring woman behind, accelerating as Steph cries in the floor of the car and Alice hisses about blame and selfishness and sacrifice and Steph curls into the far edge of the floor against the passenger door, whimpering, and her cheek is flaming red and her arm is bruised and there are strands of hair between Alice's fingers and the landscape flashes by the window and the years pass and Steph doesn't forget, won't forget, and all Alice has ever wanted is to know she is alright, to know she is safe, and Steph never, ever, understands.

What she lost then. She doesn't know what she lost then. There is no difference. Hitting or being hit. The pain is the same. There is something empty and aching in her. It's cold and sharp. It hurts in her chest when she moves.

Then, one morning, over coffee. At Steph's kitchen table. Lindy is eight months old. Steph reminds her she isn't forgiven. Sometimes she reminds her she isn't forgiven. She is calm, she is quiet. But there is a cold hatred in her eyes. It rises now and then. The look always frightens Alice when it appears.

"If you ever lay a hand on Lindy," Steph says, "that will be the end of it."

Alice's fingers tighten around her coffee cup and she stares at the tabletop. I'd never hurt you or Lindy. I love you both so much, she tells her.

"Yeah, well. . ." And Steph won't say anything else.

What she lost then. After that, she is always careful. Careful in how she moves, in what she says. After that, she smiles. And even later, when Steph asks her to babysit occasionally, she sits upright by Lindy as she twirls around the room, a six-year-old whirlwind. What she lost then, she doesn't know what she lost then.

At the top of the stairs she can't remember if her bedroom is on the left or the right. She stands gripping the banister on the landing. She is old. She feels heavy. Her limbs are heavy. Her brain is weighted in her skull. Her lungs are tight and small. She is both heavy and empty, she is so small. She makes herself so small. She tries to collect the scattered pieces of her body and make herself small.

She sits on the bed before going down to her mom. She sits on the side of the bed. She pulls up her underwear and her pants and sits very still. Her body is blasted. In pieces around her room. And still it is very small, curled tightly into itself. Her body is not a part of her. Her body is lost. It has vanished and she can't find it. She is outside her body. Just above or just behind.

Lindy brings tea. In a pretty china cup. On a saucer. Alice can see the steam rising from the cup, the string looped around the handle. Lindy puts the cup on the bedside table and sits down beside Alice on the bed, smoothing the quilt between them with her palm. She is so young. And pretty. She is so young. Pretty and sweet.

Lindy is happy Alice is dressed. She's talking about school. And soccer practice. And Gabe. Someone named Gabe. Alice can hear her, but the voice seems far away. Still, it is pleasant. The lilt and music of it. It calms her. Just having Lindy beside her for a moment on the bed. And the music of her voice. It calms her.

She stutters from her daze when the lawnmower starts. On the side of the bed. Her room is broken. The walls won't come together. There are gaps in the floor. She can see how deep the hole is, just beneath the floor. She can feel herself rocking gently on the bed. Gently. Back and forth. She can feel the movement in her body. Gently rocking. But she isn't a part of her body. She is somewhere else. She is not the one rocking with her palms between her legs.

There is blood on her fingers. Her body is cold. An empty cold. A wide and empty cold. A field of ice stained red at a faraway edge. Stained red and warm.

Lindy pats Alice's thigh, then stands up. She reminds her of the tea. "I'll be right downstairs if you need anything, G-Ma," she says.

She is bleeding. She is cold with terror. Her skin is like glass. She knows she'll shatter if she moves. She hears a car in the driveway. She turns her head slowly. Her body doesn't break. She stands up. It takes forever to stand up. It takes forever to get to the bathroom.

She takes off her pants and her stained underwear. Her limbs are heavy and her joints resist. Her hands are old. Her skin thin and spotted and her fingers won't move the way she wants them to. She has to hold to the bathroom sink, but still she can't lift her leg high enough. She has to sit on the toilet.

She hides the underwear in the bottom of the trash can in the bathroom. She hears her mother's car in the driveway. The front door opens. And closes. Alice stands in the bathroom for a very long time. She doesn't look in the mirror. She doesn't want to see herself. She doesn't look at anything.

The lawnmower is circling the house. Momma, she says. For the last time.

"Go," Momma said. She doesn't look at her.

And Alice sees that she is naked. And that is all that matters. Her nakedness. And she covers herself with her hands. She looks down at the floor, but she can't turn back up the stairs.

She knows Momma and Daddy love her. Sometimes they tell her. She wants to love them. She does love them. She loves them. But their love is so hard.

Years later, after Daddy has died and Momma has lived alone for too long, when she doesn't have a job and doesn't look pretty anymore, Alice asks her about her own childhood. Momma begins to tell her a story about a barn, a front porch, about her Daddy and her brother, then she stops. She chews her lip. She waves her hand. She says she can't remember.

"That's what women do," Momma says, after a long pause, staring at Alice. Then, she turns away: "We forget."

She wants to be invisible. She knows she isn't, can't be. She wants to be. She wants to disappear but she can't. Yet she can't appear either. She can only drift, somewhere outside her body. She floats.

She can almost see herself. Almost. And, somehow, she turns and her foot rises to the first step. To go back upstairs. Downstairs is no different from upstairs.

At the top of the stairs, the families are there. They watch her. She can hear the voices. The front door opens and closes. At the bottom of the stairs she could see into the kitchen.

Steph will be home from work. She can hear Lindy and Steph talking by the door. Steph is always so pretty when she's dressed for work.

The carpet beneath her feet. The wide staircase. The pictures on the wall. Her knees ache. Her hand slides down the banister.

Alice comes down the stairs and Momma is there, and Steph is there, and Lindy is there. And they say, Go back upstairs and put on some clothes, and they don't hear her. And Alice turns toward the stairs.

THE SPIN I'M IN

It was only a glance but it was enough to get the whole thing started. Enough to churn up a whole new possible history from the murk of who I am. Or think I am, or want to be, or can't imagine. It was only a glance but it was the kind of glance felt as a touch. His eyes shifting from the groceries, across the counter and up toward mine. The kind of glance that connects in my body, sending off sparks in all directions, making me remember my arms and legs and breasts.

And when he followed me to the door, leaving the register behind and the old man open-mouthed, that's when I turned to him, meeting his eyes for the first time. Maybe I was blushing, I don't know, but I gave him my number. Stood there catching my breath as he poked it into his phone. Forced myself not to look down when he looked up and smiled. I'll call you, he said, and he did a few hours later and I've carried his glance and his voice for a week now and, like a small child with her secret treasures, I make excuses to be alone and unveil these things again, spreading them in my lap, turning them in my fingers.

When I was pregnant with Sean, there were moments of terror. I was twenty-two, just out of college, married for a year or so. There were times I'd become paralyzed with fear at the responsibility of a new life, and I could not recover whatever beautiful dreams Mark and I had when we'd decided to become parents. My mom would attempt to soothe me.

I remember one day: it's April and we're sitting in a restaurant. We're finishing our coffee. I'm squirming, aware of this alien thing floating inside me, and I know there's something in my voice like pleading when I ask her, "Why? Why did I decide to do this? It's just too much."

And she smiles, the sort of smile I realize now all mothers reserve only for their children. Her hand slips across the table to cover mine. "Darling," she says, "with the really important things, all we can do is say yes and figure it out from there."

I think I'm going to cry: "Did I say yes?"

Mom nods gently. "You said yes."

In the kitchen, I am solid. I gather weight. In the kitchen, I know where I am. Stirring the peas, feet planted before the stove. And even if my brain flies in a hundred directions and voices crowd my head, I know my feet are below me, resting on the new tile we put in last year to replace the hideous green linoleum. I check the lasagna in the oven, I slice the bread. I don't think about last night. I stir the peas, watching intently as the butter loses shape and spreads. Last night, when the phone trembled on the table, I slipped out of bed. My hands were hot and I slipped from the room and into the hall to read his text, his text which told me I was loved and wanted, making me a real person somehow with a body someone might hold in a flash of desire. I held the phone in front of me, squatting in the hallway outside the bedroom door, bathed in blue from the tiny screen. "What in the world are you doing?" Mark asked, scuffing into the doorway behind me, absently rubbing his chin, "it's three in the morning." I snapped the phone closed. "It rang. I thought it might be an emergency, but it was just a wrong number." I stood up beside him, the hallway dark now. "Come back to bed," he said.

The peas are simmering, the lasagna resting in the oven. The phone is on the counter near the toaster. I try not to look but it tugs at my sleeve. I wash out the sink so I won't text him. Sometimes the texting helps, my single intimate signal making slow contact, quiet and invisible. Sometimes it doesn't; sometimes it just intensifies the ache like cold on a cracked tooth.

He's probably fifteen years younger. Just out of college, he says. Sharing a house with a couple of guys until he can get a real job, some kind of engineering. He's supple and warm and his smile is kind. When he touched my hand, there by the door after he'd abandoned his register, his grip was strong but his hands were smooth, unmarked and clean.

In the texts, he calls me beautiful. And sexy. Those are the words he uses. He tells me he wants to touch me. The few times we've talked, in the afternoon before everyone gets home, I feel myself drift into his voice. I know it's crazy but the conversation is easy—we use our getting-to-know-you voices—and everything is new and possible and the world could suddenly brighten to a supernova, leaving only two in its wake.

I'd flirted with him in the store, that half-serious flirting leaving just enough room for denial, just enough room to be offended if he said the wrong thing. All I really wanted was a single spark, the chance connection of stray wires touching, something to light this dark space inside me just long enough to know it's still there.

I'd noticed him before. He moves through the store like he knows what he wants. He's new, not tired. He's a mystery and I imagine his touch in the dark, his hand moving toward mine, his lips at my neck and the pressure of his breath and I come into my body again, as if it's some fragile thing fluttering softly inside this larger frame, and it's light there and calm.

He wants to meet somewhere. He wants to take me out to dinner. He wants me. If he would just say the words, the right words, my life would drop and fold into itself at my feet and I would step over it, out the door and across the lawn.

I pick up the phone. I put it down again.

The kitchen is warm. It smells good. Tomato sauce, cheese, vegetables and all the meals we've cooked since we've been in this house, eight years now. I wander from the sink and into the dining room where I can see the backyard through the two bay windows. Dry leaves clatter against the panes, filling the sky like swarms of golden birds deciding where to nest. I stare out past the swing set and the garden shed, over the fence and into the trees, the leaves trembling green in the angled light of autumn. This house smells like us. The kids when they were young, in diapers toddling chair to chair. Mark and me, growing up, figuring ourselves out. The sleepovers, the forts built under the dining room table, the stupid fights about stupid things. Soccer uniforms, gym tights, and secret diaries with a key. We're embedded in the carpet and the sheetrock. Move everything out tomorrow and we'll still be here as shadows or ghosts. The kitchen is warm, the counter warm where my hand rests open by the phone. I glance at the refrigerator and Sean's note reminds me of his game on Thursday. Twitching with a sudden chill, I pick up the phone to clear the history.

His last text comes up, the 3 a.m. text, but I don't read it; I click back one screen to the list and highlight them all, staring down at the lines floating in a block of dark blue, twenty or more just in the last week. Some kind of history happening all at once. The kind of history nobody sees coming. Like an earthquake, a drought, an accidental death.

I imagine he gets us a room and it's always a hotel. With a lobby. And I stand, in the lobby, discretely near the elevator like the heroine of a film from the 40s. I am beautiful, and he glances impatiently toward me as he completes his transaction. We're hardly on the other side of the door when he presses me back against it, his lips on mine before I speak, his hands parting my coat and sliding upward. He flattens his palms against my cheeks as we kiss and I link my hands in the small of his back and we fade into the door, into the room, fade to a thin blanket of sensation shrouding everything and he is on me and I am around him and maybe we're on the bed and maybe not but it's our room anyway, our place, and we mark it now with our screams and kisses and I am in one place, with him, one place—tall and loose-limbed and smiling—and I know where I am. I'm with him.

Or: one afternoon, his car simply sidles to a stop at the end of the walk and I'm by the car and in my doorway at the same time and he looks up to me from the steering wheel and says, I got a job in Boston … come with me. And I stand at the door, gazing down the walk to the shining red tablet of his car and sometimes it's a long path and sometimes it's accomplished with a single step but I pause long enough to write a note. I don't look back, I don't pack a suitcase or grab my credit cards, but I pause long enough to write a note to leave folded on the small table by the front door. He's waiting and my breath is quick and the car is just there and I write a note which I imagine explains everything, if not now then later when Rebecca and Sean are old enough to understand.

I flip the phone closed, hiding its light. Rebecca is perched on a stool at the kitchen island, head tilted to press her phone to her shoulder as she draws a composition book and pen from her backpack and slaps them to the counter. Rebecca is always on the phone. We pay exorbitant phone rates for an unlimited plan because Rebecca is always on the phone. I scoop lasagna and peas onto a plate and slide it across the counter toward her. She looks up when it arrives, mouthing a cockeyed thank you, then returns to her homework and the phone and dinner, alternating erratically, pausing with her fork over the plate or shrieking with her mouth full at some incredible insight inaudible to me. She dances on her stool, rocking forward and back, eating and laughing, her eyes wide with surprise then narrowing in concentration, then asking the person on the other end for the answer to number twenty-seven. And I remember her. The shape of her tiny body and the smell of her newborn hair and the way she shifts in my grasp growing lanky and sure and never saying Mommy now, her own life fanning out around her and away from me, in widening arcs.

I dream of houses, I always have. Long before this house, before my marriage, even as a child. In the dreams, I explore rooms opening to rooms, going on forever, some with furniture, ordered and clean, while others are a chaos of boxes and clothes and treasures, filling me with a sense of discovery. But, in the nightmares, I lean back against a door I've just passed through, knowing I've closed it on something which cannot follow me. The room around me is pitch black. I can feel an entire house but I'm blind to it. And I cannot bring myself to step away from the door, the only landmark I have.

I fade from the kitchen somehow, fading toward him again, losing my place, losing it to a tingling at the base of my spine as if he's touched me and a slight gasp I cover with my hand so Rebecca can't hear. Turning away, I place my hands on both sides of the sink. I fade toward him, as if another life awaits fully formed, another room I could step into, another house where I would be someone different.

But there isn't another life; there are only beginnings and endings with nothing between. I fade but he isn't there. I don't even know who he is. He's the lifeline I hold to, in the same way I hold to this room and the hope of new kitchen cabinets and proud report cards on a new refrigerator. I've faded and I struggle back, to my feet on the floor, struggling away from the blind place and toward the polished sink and kitchen counter held fast within the brittle shell of this house.

I pull him close, trying to wrap his dream around me. I fumble for his touch, but the images have lost their shape. The hotel or the car at the end of the walk. I pull him toward me and the last text where he wrote about my body, my legs, my breasts and the fullness of my lips, and the phone is vibrating on the counter but I don't want to answer it with Rebecca in the room and I can't move, can't pick it up and walk to the dining room, can only remain still, clinging to the sink, feeling myself trickle into my form slowly like wax into the molds Rebecca and I used when we made candles last year at Christmas.

A shove nearly topples me. Sean shoulders his way to the front of the stove, catching me by the arm as I tip over, laughing: "Jeez, Mom, you musta been asleep or something. You're like onea those cows the rednecks sneak up on." He pulls me toward him and I rattle against his side. He kisses me on the cheek, his breath a mixture of Sean and Cheetos and probably a surreptitious cigarette a day or two ago. His arm snakes around my shoulder as he lifts pot lids with his other hand and clatters them back atop their pots. I sink into him for a moment, hoping he doesn't notice. He's jangling spoons in the silverware drawer, talking about Biology class and the kid who got suspended for eating something he cut from a dissected frog. "It's only a rumor for now, but, knowing Kevin, I'm betting it's true." He laughs, spooning in a huge mouthful of peas directly from the pot, then dipping into the lasagna. "Don't eat like that," I nag, slapping his shoulder, "sit down and I'll fix you a plate." "Can't," he mumbles, shoving in another mouthful, "gotta be at Carrie's in ten minutes. Big calculus test tomorrow. See you later." And he's gone.

I turn to the kitchen island and Rebecca has vanished from her stool, probably dumping her books before the TV in the family room and, even though I've been alone all afternoon and hardly noticed, now that the kids have come and left, the kitchen feels large and empty. A jolt of terror clutches the base of my neck, shooting into my legs.

It's the same terror I felt the day I lost Sean at the mall. He was five and it was almost Christmas. He was sitting on the edge of a fountain staring happily into the falling water and I was on the phone and I turned on one foot the way you do when you're talking and when I spun around again he was gone.

I couldn't catch my breath. I stood by the fountain, unable to move. The crowd whirled past on both sides, their packages knocking against my legs. I stared at the spot where I'd left him as if I could will him to appear. I broke into the crowd, cutting across the current to one storefront then another, one doorway then another, spinning frantically in all directions until I finally found him, staring into a wide window where a toy train endlessly circled a single stuffed bear on clouds of cotton snow.

And something made me pause. I didn't run up and snatch him into my arms in relief or scold him for wandering off. I stood, motionless, maybe twenty feet away, watching his eyes follow the train in its circle with a complete joy, one small hand flattened to the glass. I stopped—something helped me to stop—and I saw him and his excitement, so that when I came up behind him and put my hand on his shoulder, he could look up to me with a great grin and point and we could watch the train together. And we stayed there, before the window, until he tugged at my sleeve and said he was ready to go.

I want to stop now, I want to be still. I try to be still, but I'm already in motion and I don't know where I'm going. Nothing in my life quite fits together. There are gaps showing everywhere. Gaps growing wider, revealing a nameless open space I can't bring myself to enter.

"Mom," Becca calls from the family room, "we got any ice cream?"

Mark bangs through the storm door, briefcase first, arms filled with files and his raincoat. He winks when the door slams shut and he sees me jump. He balances everything to rest near Becca's dirty plate, then shrugs from his jacket and folds it across the pile. I scoop my phone from the counter and slide it into my pocket. "I have to go to the store anyway, Bec," I call back. "I can pick some up. What kind do you want?" Mark's coming around one end of the island as I round the other. "Dinner's on the stove," I hear myself saying, "Sean's at Carrie's, I'm going out for a few things, back in a little while." I'm imagining the motion of the car and the curve of the wheel. The fracturing, wet light of dusk. The silence inside and the faint hiss of the tires on the road. I'll check my texts in the parking lot and send a reply, then delete them all. I grab my purse. Mark turns from the stove toward me, an empty plate in his hand. I catch him in the corner of my eye and swing toward him from habit, but this time I don't stop; I complete the turn, allowing some sort of faint smile as our eyes swipe each other.

And yet, I don't avoid eye contact with the man on the sidewalk outside the store. In fact, I seek it out. I'd noticed him when I entered and didn't make my usual effort to avoid panhandlers when I came out.

"Miss," he exclaims, as if calling to a small child.

I turn toward him, my bag glancing against my leg. I see him and he notices, his eyes flickering in recognition of mine. There's a slight jerk of attention between us and we adjust our posture imperceptibly. He's looking down at the cement as if it's just dropped into focus and I'm sliding along the sidewalk toward him. There's a kind of nameless anticipation in the way we come before each other.

He's older, small but wiry, his feet planted wide on the sidewalk. He's wearing a fake down coat they must have given him at the shelter, dark jeans and unlaced sneakers. He has a three-day growth of beard but his hair is short and neat. His face is weathered, deep wrinkles around his eyes and mouth; the eyes are damp, the mouth flattened into something like a grimace. His body knots and loosens in a thousand slight shifts and ripples and he struggles with his words as if they hurt his mouth.

Inside, the store had seemed abnormally bright, all the colors harsh. The glare from the floor, the stacks of canned vegetables, the bright candy wrappers, all hurt my eyes. I'd pushed my cart aimlessly up one lurid aisle after another before remembering all I needed was ice cream. I grabbed two half gallons, collecting frost on my fingertips, leaving the half-moon of a handprint on the glass door of the freezer, then I was outside, away from the light into the tart autumn night and some faltering sense of myself again in the darkness.

"Miss, I know you got no reason to talk to me.

"It's just..." he's looking at me, searching for something, "I'm tryin, I'm really tryin." He glances down at himself, his ragged shoes and restless feet, he flaps his coat open, hands in pockets, then pulls it tighter.

And all at once I know where I am. I'm alone. With only questions and a past. I want to ask him what I should do. Because we share the sidewalk, because his eyes met mine and he wants to tell me something. I want to ask him; it suddenly seems that he might have a clearer hold on something than I do. Instead, I fold a five into his palm and touch his shoulder. Take care of yourself, I say.

They're all home now, piled into the family room. Mark's leaning back in his recliner, glasses partway down his nose. He's opening files in his lap, scanning and signing off on one after another, passing them to a stack on the coffee table. Rebecca's on her back in her puddle of books, staring at the ceiling, while Sean has thrown himself onto the sofa, earbuds in place, texting furiously. And there they are, arranged around the room as a family, while I drive in circles two blocks from the house, ice cream softening in the seat next to me. If Mark could just get up from his recliner when I come into the house; if he'd just take me in his arms and hold me close, his breath in my hair, and tell me everything is going to be alright. If he would just say the right words to make me believe him. Maybe then, I could be the person I was, years ago when it first started. If we could just remember something together, then maybe our lives would pull back in place, each piece locking with the next to form a vision we could believe in. But his touch never connects anymore; it drifts or slides away before reaching my skin and even as I watch him try, I cannot push my hand toward his.

I turn, and turn again, easing up to stop signs, easing into the intersections, allowing the wheel to spin back through my fingers as the car rights itself from each turn, while I study the houses and porch lights and parked cars. Enjoying the sway of the car, the way it glides from one street to the next, humming softly to itself. Enjoying the way the houses and lawns and abandoned bicycles order themselves outside the glass. The gray-blue of the cut grass and the amber squares of the windows.

And I hear the old man's voice and his fingers

bunching in the pockets of his coat as he shifts foot to foot in something like embarrassment at his sudden need to tell a truth about himself, as if he just has to accomplish it this one time and it will be over and done with. He's as twisted and torn as a flag round a post. When I touch his shoulder, I feel his body tight and hot beneath the cushion of his coat.

He stares down at the tongues of his sneakers, slowly lifting one foot then the other. My hand slips from his shoulder. His eyes are welling when they meet mine. "Mom and Pop, they took me to church," his coat flaps open again, "I was raised better. They showed me the right way. And I... I..."

It's only a glance but it's enough to get the whole thing started. Enough to churn up a whole new history from the murk of who I am. Or think I am, or want to be, or can't imagine. It's only a glance but it's the kind of glance felt as a touch.

I don't realize I'm crying until tears drop to my lap but once I notice, the tears overwhelm me. My chest heaves and I hear myself sob. It's loud and seems to come from another place, outside the car, in the air somewhere. I ease to a stoplight and put the car in park. I listen to the sobs, low and dark as distant blasts, my body shuddering, my fingers opening and closing over the skin of the wheel.

I don't know why I'm crying, I don't know what I'm crying about, but it's something beyond disappointment or loss. It's old and sharp and has its own voice. I'm crying in another language, a language I'd known once but have forgotten.

My hand slips from the old man's shoulder and I turn away from him into the night, turning away to hide my emotion, turning away so I won't ask a question.

"I know what God looks like," he mutters to his shoes, but he's watching me as I turn to leave. I glance back and our eyes meet again. "I know what God looks like, Miss," he calls after me as I walk away. "He looks like you."

◆ ◆ ◆

Mark tells me my mother's been calling because she couldn't get me on the cell. It's only then I discover I've left the phone on the front seat of the car. He's undressing on his side of the bed while I sit on mine, staring in front of me, raw and empty from the tears in the car which he hasn't noticed. Mark tells me I should call my mom. Okay, I reply. There's a sudden silence. He's stopped moving behind me. "Franny, are you okay?" he asks, and I can hear the care and love in his voice and I know that if I turn I'll see the way that care and love tunnels back, growing wider and deeper, to the moment we met and I'll know I love him, and it's not enough. I'm fine, I call back, crossing the few feet to the bathroom door and closing it behind me. I don't turn on the light. I want the darkness. I press myself against the door. All I can see is the outline of my feet in the crease of light at the floor. I want to move but I can't; I want to shout or scream, or explain myself, but there's only one thing left to say.

And it's already been said.

PILGRIMS

The stars thinned to arcs circling our heads, blurring into strokes or scratches carved into the empty blue-black sky. We spun in the gallery parking lot, arms held out, staring up, concentrating so as not to trip over our own feet, arms held out, passing over or under the other's most times then striking, glancing off, the contact bumping us slightly in our orbits. Stumbling into each other, we continued to stare up, giggling low and throaty, keeping it going as long as we could, spinning with the night blurring around us, spinning with the loose sensation of earth beneath our feet but only etched sky in our vision. We kept it going until we fell into each other, clutching at shoulders and arms to keep from falling, stumbling sideways, the earth tilting around us, legs a tangle but not falling, catching ourselves and each other and not falling, managing somehow to stay afoot until we came to a stop gasping, one and the other, hunched over, hands on our knees staring at our shoes in the gray fading light, our shoes which, when they finally settled into place beneath us, seemed very far away.

Sarah's forehead rested on my chest, damp, warm as the night air. I slid my hand down her bare arm and left it there.

"We're dervishes!" she announced breathlessly.

"Not very good ones," I countered.

She squeezed my hand, tugging me toward the sidewalk: "Well, you've got to start somewhere."

Years later, I can't enter a gallery without remembering the night, the parking lot, and standing beside her one painting after the next. I didn't know anything about art; I'd only ever cared about basketball and guitar. We were twenty-one or twenty-two and Sarah wasn't older, she just seemed clearer somehow. I stood beside her, the crowd fading around us; I stood beside her and tried to see what she saw.

And at the door of every gallery since, I lose my place for an instant, slipping into the rush of that night, the current which seemed to condense our eccentric dance and the unfathomable thing between us then and forever into a gesture:

Sarah separates from me, her head lifting from my shoulder. I reach out to hold the door for her. She approaches, my back against the opened door, she comes up close and I think she's going to kiss me there in the gallery entrance. Instead, her hand slips into my back pocket and she squeezes, then she turns me with the slip of her hand around her in the open door; she spins me gently around her axis and follows me, squeezing again, sliding into place at my side.

Rotating around her like a car on a carnival ride, I remember her stance before the blank, white canvas and the way the work changed shape one day to the next; layers applied, scraped, applied again, gathering and burning off like dew.

And for an instant I know faith is something that's already happened, something I only catch up to afterward. A simple gesture or a few words sparking into a flicker of recognition before vanishing again into the folds of life.

It was Sarah that night, only Sarah, climbing the stairs with me, just before the door and after our spin in the parking lot, our bodies still lurching into each other in the remnants of vertigo. She found the gesture, completed it.

"Oh, you can't miss us," the receptionist replied when I asked for directions, pulled as I am to galleries, years later, by the impressions Sarah left on my skin. "We're the glass and steel wedge between the restaurant supply warehouse and the constant construction." She adds: "When you get here, make sure you start on the third floor and work your way down. That's how you're supposed to do it anyway."

So I make an afternoon of it, the trip to the Bowery. I take the subway and wander the streets aimlessly in the light gray drizzle framed by gray buildings. When I arrive, the threshold is enough to recall Sarah and that first gallery.

We slid into the building that night bodies all aflutter in the bright light and the neutral carpet and the evening gowns and dinner jackets with Sarah in her red silk dress, towering in her heeled alligator boots, trailing various glittering scarves. She looked like Ziggy Stardust's orphan sister. I followed, a satellite in her orbit, as she swept into the crowd, scooped two glasses of red wine from the table and spun back, offering one in an extended hand.

"Welcome to the world of Art!" she declared, and she was only half joking. "I mean, look at this," she exclaimed, turning the stem between her fingers, "They use real glasses."

We paraded through the exhibition, pausing before each painting, continuing once she'd managed a grunt or moan. She held her glass precariously between two fingers, her arm rising and falling with her attention. I'd watch her study them, head tilting to one side, light rising in her eyes as she took a few steps back or moved closer to inspect a twinge of color.

We hadn't gone far when someone shrieked her name, she spinning in the direction of the voice, leaning toward it instinctively and away from me, fingers sliding from my arm, head angling back as she mouthed, "Just a minute," then sailed away to throw her arms around a tall elderly woman with even taller hair.

I hummed in her absence, a top left to wobble in place. I circled the gallery alone, uncovering a gentler stream which brought me close to one painting after another. I'd linger there, trying to enter her joy in color and shadow, trying to imagine the feeling she had with a brush in her hand.

I could see her behind me now and then, all hummingbird flutter and laugh, bobbing bloom to bloom, some wild virus of light coursing through the room. Now and then, her hand returned to my back pocket and she'd knead my cheek for a moment like a kitten settling into a purr.

Lips near my ear, she'd whisper, "Death to everyone but us." It was the kind of thing she'd say when we found ourselves doing something that made sense only to the two of us: spending our last few dollars on theater tickets, or driving nine hours in one of our dubious cars to see a band.

Now and then, she kisses me. Always bringing me back to the doorway, her hand in my pocket, slipping in just as I pull open the door, her fingers closing. An act so casually intimate that gravity ceases and I drift, dislodged from my body somehow, watching as we turn.

In today's gallery, I follow a presence of light in the canvases, follow the way it filters one to the next. The work on the third floor, blue gold and dusky, gives way to darker pieces on the second, rooms cut hard into sections of brightness and dark, frames mostly black save an angled shadow falling upon an essential form. I move one to the other the way a cat follows sunlight. I drift, renewing a faith discovered so long ago.

Sarah. Standing in a corner of her studio, her cramped, cluttered studio; freezing in winter, stifling in summer, only a space heater for one season and a single functional window in the skylight for the other. The warm, rank smell of paint and linseed oil, sweat, and a fine, damp dust.

She'd stand beside a covered easel held together by wire, the loose ends budding from the top in sharp fronds. One hand at the stained sheet, the other on her hip, she'd blow a few strands of dark hair from her face. She'd pull back the sheet, her bare arm settling along the top edge, her attention fixed upon me as my eyes darted from one corner of the canvas to another, spilling over the image.

A smile would spread across her face; I'd see it at the edge of my vision not overwhelmed by paint, light and shadow. She'd watch me, bending one leg at the knee, resting her foot on the toe.

I'd flush, unsure, while she remained patient, learning as much from my body as any words I found. There was no thinking to be done; there was only color, movement, and sound. I'd smile, a different smile every time. She'd understand something then but I never knew what. She'd lower her eyes to the floor. Perhaps she was smiling then too, her head slightly declined, but I never knew since I was caught in the burn before me, one color and stroke flowing around the next, changing the light in the room. The way a painting can change the light in a room.

I liked to watch her as she worked. Her surroundings would fall away from her once she began. I could sit on a stool by the sink with my guitar and the ancient gurgling coffee pot, and glimpse her through the shutter of the easels, standing before the blank white, turning this way and that, brush first at shoulder height then gradually falling to her waist, rising slightly then sinking away while she swayed before the canvas as if finding a breeze.

With a single stroke, something would lighten in her body, one foot lifting from the floor for an instant, the fingers of her left hand curling, and she'd stand absolutely still in the posture of an exotic bird. I'd glance up to find her poised there, brush arrested an inch from the canvas, and I'd watch until she found the next stroke, settling gently back to earth, one foot touching down then the other.

We lived on box wine, ramen, crackers and peanut butter, splitting our time between our cramped apartments, gathering change every Friday for a night out, attending any gallery opening or reception where there might be free drinks and shrimp, our married friends occasionally taking pity on us, inviting us over for a real meal. Our cars were held together with wire and hope, our clothes harvested from yard sales and Goodwill. She was a waitress and I was a security guard; she spent every cent on paint and canvas while I blew mine on obscure records and effects pedals.

She'd come to see me, in pick-up bands I found now and then, being too obnoxious and full of myself to ever be a member of anything for long. She'd sit in a corner on a stool or old crate she'd found, closing her eyes, swaying in the music, fingers articulating a gentle curve in the air. She'd pull me to her side after, saying nothing. She held a silence for me, a silence I could share for an instant before it faded.

It was a silence we discovered when she led me into her studio for the first time, a sweltering night in August when she threw the door open and took me by the hand, drawing me through the maze of canvas and easels, then releasing me, turning in the failing blue light overhead, turning toward me, her eyes on mine, unbuttoning her shirt. It was a silence birthed the moment I reached out and flattened my palm in the pale, warm hollow between her breasts.

Years later, I still call her studio to mind with a kind of idiot reverence. The room had its own weather. It was a climate composed of color and the sound one color makes sliding along, or flowing over, another: the lilt of reds along blues, the deep angle of an earth tone into green, the rumble of blacks and grays, sometimes nearly hidden beneath the rustle of the helicopter breeze from the slow overhead fan.

I come to rest again before the large painting on the ground floor near the gift shop, having made two orbits of the exhibit. More people have arrived and there's a wave-like hush in the building now. They bring a kind of white noise rumble akin to the sound in a hall just before the performance begins, the low anticipatory hum of engines settling to a low idle.

There's something gently churning in the reds and the low rhythm where they flow along the band of blue. The sounds rise into the wash of the room around me. It could be mistaken for silence but it's too vital. Much like a music played two rooms away, it draws me toward it.

It's the kind of active stillness I could never find in a bar or club, where the audience always seemed the enemy, the obstacle to overcome. Where I always felt I was pushing every chord out into noise and chaos, hoping it might survive, somewhere out there, away from me, just beyond sight. Hoping it might cut through the uproar and demand its own attention. It was the stillness I was always searching for in the music, the stillness I could only struggle to approach.

The halls have grown over the years, becoming larger, quieter. But only because of the moment when suddenly, finally, there was nothing to struggle against. When the absence overtook me, I vanished. There was only music and the guitar. When it happened, it wasn't my playing that changed, it was my listening. The thing I'd feared most was what I most wanted:

It's another shitty night in a shitty bar and something about the five layers of shit, on this Tuesday or Thursday or whatever it is, breaks something loose and I play in a way I've always known in my bones but could never reach, breathing some kind of clearer breath where the inhalation and the exhalation are extended for minutes and the space between each opens into a stillness which has no time and in that stillness, music pushes into me like some kind of deep slow kiss, the band careening behind me, a shambling trailer hitched to my guitar.

Something happens that night, something wandering comes to rest. Feet apart, the back of the guitar sliding along my thigh, I have no sensation of fingers on strings, the music finally becoming for me a thing that simply exists. With me, around me.

I glance out over the bobbing heads of the crowd toward the stark lights at the back of the bar. A couple dances there, slow and calm. I know it must be Sarah and me. We're locked together, turning, my arms at her waist, her hands in my back pockets, her head on my shoulder. It's our last night together and we know it.

It's very hot. Our shirts cling to our skin. We smell like wet llamas and that's okay. She's left the music on somewhere near the back of the room and Sam Cooke is singing. He seems very happy.

We're roughing out our own song, a shadow pulse in our bodies. We feel it move one limb to the next. We strain to hear the next note, hoping it might reveal itself, but our verses are always ending in ellipsis now, our choruses just tears and sighs. All we can keep is the rhythm, of her blood and mine, the shuffle of our feet along the gritty floor, the soft release of our tears.

I no longer remember the last argument, the last slammed door. I remember our last night and the long dry ache which followed. I remember the drift of her paintings wall to wall in the angled light from the high windows, then the blue light failing above us as we held each other in the center of the room, standing, rocking slightly, articulating the slowest dance in the world; both of us crying, hot, hurt, aching and raw; both of us crying, our cheeks pressed to each other, our lips chapped and salty; holding each other because there was nowhere else to go, extending some private pain we knew belonged to us and only us, holding each for comfort but also to keep that exquisite ache alive for a few moments longer. We stayed up all night that night. We found ourselves on a street corner bench, sagging into each other as the sun slipped back into the sky.

We dance as I play. We're hardly moving at the far edge of the crowd. My hand comes up to touch her hair, her fingers tighten in my pockets in response. Her stillness is my stillness and it reaches around us and beyond us and the music is there, far from me somehow but very close, mine but not mine. Somehow I have vanished while the space my body fills is bright and electric.

On the first floor, the canvas opens itself, filling my field of vision. The fresh notes surrendered by each previous painting fade as the larger work somehow completes here, in the low horizon line and the swell of a deep red turning around something darker, the gait of its melody just audible. The opening chords on my skin, my fingers thrum my thigh softly as I tease them out.

I know it now, each shade sliding into place around the bright core of a melody. I know it clearly, note by note. I feel her in the room; I feel her in me.

She's watching from near the gift shop. She doesn't speak until I turn. She's older now but there's still paint under her fingernails. A smile curls onto her lips and her voice is low and quiet: "Billy. You've always got a song going don't you?"

"Can't help it," I tell her, sweeping my hand over the room, "they're everywhere." I take a deep breath. "I didn't think you'd be here. Thought I could sneak in and out."

"Normally I wouldn't be. But there's a fundraiser this evening." Behind her, two guys are tipping folding tables upright. A trolley for glasses and a warming cabinet are pushed against the wall. "Just a meet and greet. Sign a few catalogs, schmooze the bluehairs." Sarah winks: "Wait around long enough, there'll be wine . . . and shrimp."

An elderly couple passes between us, murmuring, heads tilted into each other.

"This is great, you know," I exclaim with a schoolboy enthusiasm, "you've got the whole place to yourself."

She can't help but laugh. "I look around, well . . . it makes me happy." Her body trembles with a crisp voltage and she gives a mighty shrug to release it. "It's like, I don't know . . . welcome to the inside of my head!" It's my turn to laugh. Then, she's afraid she's said too much. She takes a long breath, staring at her boots. "I heard you were gonna to be in town, playing a few shows at Poisson Rouge."

"Were you going to come?"

"Thought about sneaking in and out."

I nod distractedly, realizing both the question and the answer are unnecessary, aware of the swarm and rush of the painting behind me, my fingers still plucking at its infant melody. I wait until she's beside me to turn toward it.

"This is my favorite," I tell her. "It dances."

"Took me years to finish it. I mean, years." She lowers her head. She might be smiling. "Just kept putting it away, trying to forget it, then bringing it back out because it wouldn't turn me loose."

We are inches apart and inches away. Her foot comes up on the toe and she reaches out as if to touch the paint. But she doesn't.

I have to ask: "Want to have coffee? Tea? A very stiff drink? I found a handful of change under the sofa cushions, we can have a big night."

"We'll have to walk eight blocks before there's anything decent."

I turn so I can see her face. The rippling bloom of the canvas is in her eyes. "Nothing wrong with that."

I wait by the door. The drizzle has eased but the glass is still wet, muffling the sounds of the street and smearing the passing figures to diminishing colors. I wait for Sarah because she leaned toward me, her lips close, her breath on my neck. I thought she might kiss me. But she didn't.

I'm about to tell her I'll come back once the event is over.

"Let's go now. . ." she whispers in a voice which may be soundless, a secret tremor I recognize, which recognizes me. "Death to everyone but us."

WILL OF A VOLCANO

She is standing on a hill. No, it's a doorway, she is in a doorway. It is night. Almost night. Dusk. And the cobblestones are wet. Though the rain stopped an hour before.

You can see the way dusk collects. Darkening the sky from the sills and rooflines outward. As if darkness were wicking into the air from the buildings, from deep underground. You can see her in the doorway.

I can see her in the doorway. Something about her is in motion. She's not leaning against the archway, though you might think so at a casual glance. Not leaning. She's swaying, just slightly. As if in a quiet music.

She's listening to the rain. No, it's stopped raining. She's listening to the emptying gutters. The storm drains beneath her feet. Or the quiet tap of a droplet hitting a smooth stone nearby. Just to her left, or her right. Above her head or around the corner.

Or, perhaps, she's imagining the shape of the puddle, the ripple of each drop slipping outward. With a kind of lilt in her shoulders and the tilt of her head. As if each ripple sounds quietly through her musculature.

You can hear the steady tap. I can hear the tap. Something rounded, a sound that seems to bloom and hold for an instant. Two taps, a drop and a bounce, then a pause as the sound hovers. Before being swallowed by the night.

The rhythm gets into my skin. Awakening something in my skin. Some image or instance I grope for, eyes closed in an attempt to draw it forth and capture it. We familiarize ourselves, this rhythm and I. In the way I might stand perfectly still then slowly extend my hand toward the muzzle of an inquisitive dog.

I wait and it comes. But not as a revelation in a blinding flash, more as a slow dissolve into sunlight. A warm, bright summer sunlight pouring through the windows onto the hardwood floor around me.

I'm shirtless and she's lying on my chest. She's shirtless on my chest. Skin to skin. Still, but not asleep; still in the sunlight. And I can feel her heartbeat in my body, faster than mine. A double rhythm.

A tapping at the cage of my chest. It might be a bird at a window, or the knock at a distant door, or a steady constant stride, one foot then another. Her heartbeat against mine, her skin against mine. I extend my arms along the bright floorboards, the muscles along my shoulders and neck lengthening, growing taut. I feel the nest of her hair at my chin. A single errant strand tickling my nose. Tempting me to lift my arms from the floor.

I know the sound of her pulse from long ago. As if I was born with its constancy. Carrying it dormant and deep.

At first it isn't a sound. I don't know it as a sound. Instead it is a presence. A pressure. A thin border growing thinner. The way a child might press his hand into a balloon, the membrane tight around her fingers, aware, the entire time, of how thin the skin of the balloon is.

It's a pressure we don't talk about for weeks. My wife and I. It's not that we put it off, avoid it. It's that there are no words. Only the pressure, becoming a sound. Becoming a rhythm. We have to find the words. We don't know how to find the words.

We've never spoken before. Not like this.

A rise and fall like a wave near shore. The sound of it in our ears. The slow steady thump of a drum. The kind you might hear when the parade is still blocks away. The kind that seems to remain always at the same distance, until suddenly it's upon you.

We're restless, trembling in a pleasant confusion. We smile at each other then turn away to smile again. We make love then throw ourselves from the bed into the yard or the car. Making love is no longer enough.

We drive in circles. Arms out the window in the night rain. Driving to be driving. Or we lie in the damp grass. Staring at nothing, talking about nothing. But staring and talking just the same.

Listening as the tap of the rhythm grows closer. This sound we somehow recognize. Like the slow ringing of a bell.

Or the dropping of rain onto a smooth concave stone. Like the slow ringing of a bell. Each peal drawing attention to the silence between. A silence vibrant, and bracing. A silence absolute, before the next droplet.

She's waiting for someone. You can see she's waiting for someone. I can see it. In the doorway. On the wet street.

Not a doorway in Paris. Or Lisbon. Not a famous doorway, or a historical one. Just a simple doorway. In any town.

Now. Last week. Last month. Now.

She might be waiting for someone. Her eyes nearly closed. Still swaying. A lover. A friend. She might be going home. Or leaving home for the night.

She might be excited. We might feel it if we were close enough. If we were standing beside her, we might sense her exhilaration. A kind of warming current in her limbs. A kind of ecstatic breathlessness. A thrill of anticipation.

Something is changing in her blood. She's waiting for

something to begin. As she waits, she discovers another sound, gently clothed within the first, the droplets of water upon the cool stone. She discovers a breeze like a whisper.

It's a slight, breathy sound. Almost not there. It's as if she's created this sound simply by noticing it. It's the thought of a breeze, the precursor to the breeze itself. It's the gesture of a breeze she hears.

In the beginning, she's wearing a red dress. Then it's gray. Now, it's blue. It's a simple dress falling just above her knee. Light stockings. Her hair is pulled back. Her hair might be black, or perhaps it's the light. She might be any age.

Dusk is gathering the light toward itself. The shadows lengthen, growing deeper. She hasn't been waiting long. For her lover. Or her friend. Or perhaps, simply for a taxi. She hasn't been waiting long.

There's a confidence in her. In her limbs. Noticing the thinnest of breezes nested inside the silence. Something as strong and unwavering as the cobblestones at her feet. There are things about herself she has always known. As clear and predictable as the positions of stars.

I turn to my wife, fingers loose on the steering wheel. The road is a dark ribbon, undulating gently. The road is empty.

The windows are open. We like the noise of the wind, the sense of motion. The roar of the night. In the car it seems we are doing something. Even if we aren't.

She's slumped in her seat. Arm extended, out the open window. We had been talking. We were talking. Work, recipes, new music to buy.

My heart is racing. With the words we haven't said over the last weeks. It's a game we're playing together. A game of approach and hesitation, of tenderness and silence and near silence.

With a new sense of closeness. Something in the last weeks drawing us together quietly, placing us together in a strange, clean light. Alternately nurturing and terrifying, with a logic available only in dreams.

We start awake. I reach across the back of the seat and slide my hand into her hair. At the back of her neck. The strands slipping into my fingers. It's a sound like the falling of paper. She rolls her head back, along my hand.

She tilts her head to look at me. Eyes nearly closed. But the moment is too tender. She turns back to the road.

"You know," I tell her, watching the road myself, "if we want to have a baby . . . I think that would be a great thing."

And, once it is said, a hundred other conversations order themselves before and after. As if we've already talked about it. As if the conversations were accomplished in our silence, in our intimacy, in the dark. In the car. Or on the lawn.

Each word we never spoke, close and clear as memory, each word we will speak unfolding in all directions, all our words suddenly present in our limbs, jumbled and stewing and sparking in their own joyous chorus. Everything, before and after, placed for an instant, within us.

I'm simply voicing the decision already made. There is a patience in this, the decision already made. We step into a new skin. It comes with a voltage in our limbs. It comes with a certain thrill, like a seduction. Only deeper and finer.

She's crying now, a murmur of weeping, soft tears hanging in her eyes before trickling down her cheek as she tilts her head when I laugh and she laughs, glancing to me for an instant before I close my hand at the back of her neck and she reaches up and behind to clasp her hand over mine and we listen, for a moment, to the whir of the tires on the road and the wind whistling by our heads and the tenor of crickets in the trees as we pass.

And she wakes me. Shaking my shoulder. Calling my name.

"It's time," she says.

And I start awake, sitting up in bed, my limbs unwired

and unmoored. I bunch my fingers into the sheets to place myself. She's sitting on her side of the bed, facing away from me, breathing hard.

"Are you sure?" I ask, because I need to say something.

"I'm sure."

A whirlwind catches us; me pulling on my pants, hopping on one leg then the other, looking around for my shoes forgetting my socks; she scuffing toward the bathroom one last time before the car then pulling her nightgown over her head and sitting on the bed again, naked, to catch her breath before standing, opening the dresser.

We move in two different currents of time, she and I; she is slow and constant, stopping often to rest, to breathe, while I collect things from one room then the next, searching for the bags we'd packed, the items we'd collected, which had been resting by the door for a week now, but I forget that somehow, searching room to room before I find them exactly where we left them.

I stop to watch her for an instant, in the doorway, before going outside to start the car and warm it against the December night. And though her body is heavy and full, there's a lightness around her, something airy and soft, like the threads of a feather or a tender leaf, a thing so real it seems outside her skin, more corporeal than her body. Steady and unafraid.

We're in the car and, even though it's winter, she's too warm, opening the window an inch so the bitter wind sweeps around us. There's heat steaming from her body in humid waves.

The road is empty, the world is empty. No cars. No lights in the windows of the passing houses. The world is patient.

We don't talk. Or we talk. It doesn't matter. She's breathing through pursed lips. An extended inhalation. Short, forceful exhalations. She's gripping my hand between us, her fingers tightening then releasing, tightening then releasing.

I'm spread-eagled on the hardwood floor, papers extended in one hand, pen in the other. I'd been sitting cross-legged, writing in my lap when she toddled over and threw herself at me, onto my lap, toppling us both, me falling back, she holding to my chest, giggling, squirming into me, babbling nonsense words of love.

Before: she doesn't crawl, she doesn't want to crawl. She wants to be carried. Facing outward, high. She wants to see everything. Everything I see.

The idea of crawling makes her furious. She refuses to try. In a month or two she'll hoist herself by the edge of the table. Until then, I hold her, I carry her. In a month or two, she'll leave the edge of the table and take her first steps toward me.

It bubbles up into her from the floor, from the hardwood floor, the box of the house, the earth beneath. This force of movement. Something invisible. Inevitable as a sunrise.

And once she understands what is happening, she'll falter, tipping forward to her hands on the floor, edging on all fours, but not crawling, toward the sofa to hoist herself again then walk the length of the room toward me with such open-mouthed wonder I can't help but shout in the shock it is to see the moment as it happens.

And my shout startles her, eyes wide then smiling, but it doesn't stop her. She doesn't stop until she collapses into my open arms.

Now, she rolls from my bare chest to place her feet on the floor then pushes herself away from me, upright. She takes the pen from my extended hand and puts it in her mouth. I rattle the pages in my other hand, but she doesn't want them. She steals my pen and walks into the kitchen. I tilt my head backward, watching her navigate the ceiling as she disappears beyond the threshold.

Later, there's the tapping of her feet across the hardwood floor in the other room. I'm at my desk. Her mother is in the kitchen. Her footsteps move steadily across the length of the living room floor then stop. My hands rest on the loose pages before me.

I know she's standing at the wide window, peering into the yard. At a bird or a bicycle or a falling leaf. I lift my hands from the desk in the silence and a sheet of paper rustles to the floor.

I hear her giggle and shout. Then the cadence of the footsteps again, across the room, to the other window, and a new scene.

At first, it isn't a story. I don't know it as a story. Instead it seems a pressure. A presence. A dream voice in another tongue. And in the dream, I turn my head this way and that, unable to find the direction of the speaker. In the dream I resign myself to waiting.

She waits, in the doorway. Expectant. Her waiting is not idle. Her waiting is a declaration. She's defining herself somehow. Shaping the next moments, the next days, with a measured patience. Something is changing in her blood.

We find the next moment together, she and I.

I'll watch her take the next step. We will see it happen. The moment in which stillness becomes motion, waiting becomes decision. We can watch from here.

The drip of the rain slows. Above her head or around the corner. The whispering breeze fades as the last lazy currents sluice through the storm drains beneath her feet. The water drains off, leaving the cobblestones slick with moisture. The night is black now, and silent.

She steps onto the street with a decisive turn. No. She stays where she is. Headlights sweep her legs, the dark wall and the glistening cobblestones. A brief fan of light across her bare legs and arms, her upturned face, tilting now toward the light.

Something changes in her eyes. There's a smile. She steps out of the archway and down to the curb.

SENSE OF PLACE

I open my eyes, not quite knowing where I am. Knowing the car, knowing the wheels beneath me. Opening my eyes to the road, to a dark and foreign road unfolding before me. The hiss of the tires, the featureless night. I open my eyes just enough to place myself. In the car beside Caleb.

The car is thick with sleep. And the heat rising from the pink, spindly limbs of the girls, snoring softly in the back seat. Suits still damp, sandals still sandy. All of us sun-baked, hot-skinned and drowsy, our clothes pricking us in tender places.

It has its own uncertain poetry; the night, the car, the road. A blurred and formless comfort. Something anticipatory, not yet accepted; a question asked yet left unanswered, not abandoned but held in pause.

Caleb has turned the radio on low and rolled down his window, which means he's getting sleepy. A late-night breeze spins through the car. I should keep him company, but I don't want to sit up in the seat. I don't want talk. I want to drift where I am, loose and liminal, riding the unseen waves of the road.

Earlier in the evening, Abby and Meghan had recounted the trip to each other in the back seat. Meghan taking the lead, then Abby joining in with her older sister: the way the sand squished between their toes when a wave slid in, the dolphins we'd spotted from the balcony, the holes dug and castles built, the surfers. They traded memories back and forth. Occasionally, they'd draw me in. Remember that, Momma? Do you remember?

Later, Meghan read to Abby, she in her seatbelt, Abby in her car seat. She tilted the picture books in Abby's direction page by page and plucked another from the stack in the seat. Then, just before sleep, they began to whisper, voices low and giggly, the pauses between them sometimes so long it was impossible to tell whether they were speaking from dream. The landscape beneath the road shifted from the still surface of sand to gentle curves and swells. The sun dropped beyond the trees and we fell asleep, leaving Caleb to navigate us, through tiny towns on two-lane highways, back to our lives.

Eyes closed, there is only motion and the slight sway of the breeze. Eyes closed, everything in me slows and settles into my breath. My breathing steady, it's a sense of place I feel. Or of being placed.

Caleb sighs and the car begins to slow, coming to a halt, and I know we're at the singular stoplight of a small town. There's something familiar in the thrilled stillness of the night. The pause. Caleb releases a slow breath. I hear the stoplight click to red above us.

The stoplight clicks to red. Alex is standing in the intersection under the light at Washington and Elm. I'm on the sidewalk. It's four in the morning, maybe five. I'm twenty or twenty-one. Alex raises his arms in a ridiculous hieratic gesture and lets out a slow, sensual moan.

We'd seen a band at the Blind Tiger. I can't remember the band, only that the music had been loud, slow, complex, building to great washes which broke over

our heads and that Alex had closed his eyes for most
of the show, swaying in his hips, arms loose at his sides
and I stood awkwardly beside him, trying to find my
place, trying to find a way to enjoy what I knew I was
enjoying, trying to voice that joy in my body.

"My God. My God! Can you believe what we just
heard?" he'd shouted in the parking lot, his body still
jointless, spasming from the music. "Man, I can't go
home now," he declared. "I need to walk. Will you
walk with me?"

I'd call this memory but it's not really that at all: it's
simply a part of me, something vital threaded through
sinew and bone. It opens all at once and I'm captured
in its fine strands, in the way I'm often stolen away by
something behind me. I'll lose the now altogether to
some shadow, not completely the present while not
exactly the past, the real trick of the past being that it
isn't the past at all; I bring every moment of it forward
with me.

We'd had a lot to drink earlier, Alex and I, but that
was wearing away now, leaving a quiet softness in its
wake. Somehow, without making the decision, we walk
away from the bars and the ragged noise of campus,
toward downtown. There are treelined residential
streets and blocks of warehouses or empty building. It
had rained while we were in the club. The road glistens,
all the colors of the night a little smeared. The trees drip,
a random droplet plunking our shoulder or splattering
in our hair. The only sound is an occasional passing car
sliding by us with a hiss.

We walk and talk. About anything. Everything.
At first, it's Alex, in great surges of words, sentences
muscling forward, jumping track, colliding with others.
He talks in a rush of excitement, beginning with the night
and the music, but sweeping everything in his path, as if
attempting to house all the world within his sentences.
Gradually this enthusiasm infects me, or wears at my
defenses, until I match his exaltations with my own.

He tells me about an eighth-grade teacher who acknowledged him, captured him, nurtured him. About a school field trip to a museum a few years later where he'd found one painting so completely alive he wanted to remain before it for hours. He tells me about the new Godspeed You! Black Emperor album, the earthy, resonant churn of the music.

"It's like a kind of message from another world," he tells me. "And I don't have to understand it, 'cause I know it already."

I drift in the gap between my guarded self and the certainty of my own joys. I'd moved from the hinterlands to the big city for college and, in my second year, having thawed from my freshman awe, I desperately want to be somebody, anybody, other than who I am. Yet, it's strangely liberating, drafting in Alex's ecstasy, to tell him of my own. My sentences begin in a familiar place but veer into the unexpected, or the ground drops beneath them and I find myself scrambling for something higher or more solid.

We walk and walk. We talk. I tell him things about myself I don't know; at least, not until they are said. There are no tragic or shameful secrets. Instead, we find a vocabulary of wonder to share. Something birthed in the gravity of the music. Some call answered between us, taken up between us. Without thought, without thinking.

I tell him about standing beneath a bracing waterfall, the icy water battering me until my body was made of mist and spray. Of watching my grandmother cook a meal, her wide hands mixing biscuits, her fingers tender with the dough as she dropped soft clumps to the metal sheet. The way her meals warmed and soothed me. I tell him about hearing Patti Smith's *Horses* for the first time.

We're tired. Our bodies steamed in the heat of the club and the press of others against us, our limbs weak from standing, swaying in the buffeting force of the music. It's very late or very early and we walk, though our calves ache and we are thirsty, walking because we're caught in this communion, something strange and unexpected yet embraced completely.

There are silences also, deep silences that the hush of the night only deepens. And for a moment it seems every word shared has made this vibrant silence possible. We've lured each other into stillness.

When we turn the corner from Market to Elm, Alex's eyes glitter. "This way," he says, "I want to see trains."

The sidewalk shines in the rain. The street is black, still water, an occasional splash of neon rippling its surface. The storefronts are dark or dimly lit, a hollow, abandoned space next door to an inviting store hung with bright dresses, lined with rainbow rows of shoes. The store aisles are vacant, the restaurant tables empty. We've emptied ourselves with our words, now every nerve ending sparks and dances. The night around us is nearly painful. The fact of a city street, the fact of another human being; it's overwhelming.

We stand at the tracks, peering down the carved path of the rails in both directions, first one then the other. We wait, side by side. And we are quiet then, a pleasant exhaustion rising in us, giving our body weight again where the words before had made us light. We wait patiently for one train, then another; the first a short passenger, its windows revealing sleepy or sleeping faces; the second an enormous freight train, cars rocking by in all colors and shapes. When the last car is out of sight and the rails no longer tremble, we turn back up Elm.

At the corner of Washington and Elm, I realize Alex is no longer at my side. He's standing in the center of the intersection, his arms raised to the night sky. The stoplight clicks to red. He lets out this low, sensual moan, something sated and tremulous. I feel his moan in my body, outward into my fingers and toes, and I can't help but smile, then laugh. He cocks his head toward me, a crooked grin playing on his face. And his face is so open and guileless, his eyes so clear, he's so completely himself before me, that there is no response but love.

I can't help but love him and love him completely. I imagine this is the instant painters anticipate before their subjects, waiting patiently for the flash when masks fall away to reveal a true face.

It's the moment Abby sees the ocean for the first time, coming to a full stop as she crests the dune. She doesn't know she's motionless. She thinks she's still running but she's completely still for an instant before she raises her arms above her head, shouting something—not words, something before words or above words—then running to the surf just to her ankles, squealing and dancing back. It's something more than love.

It's the incidental, shattering glance with a stranger on the street, the moment our eyes accidentally meet and we haven't had a chance to hide. Open and unguarded, we see into each other for an instant. And we know each other, all at once. A shock of recognition. It's nothing but adoration. A form of worship.

I want to hold the moment of seeing forever. I want to study Alex's face the way I might kneel before a beautiful painting, the way I might grow completely stilled in the face of music. I want to take it into myself in gasps as I might a mountaintop view or an open sunrise.

The blue night is easing toward morning. The flat, empty lanes extend in each direction. I can see the indigo sky and ridges of cloud in the corridor between buildings. The stoplight clicks to green and Alex extends his hand, his palm upturned and open. I step down from the sidewalk.

We've been shedding skins, all evening, with each step, with every word. And though we'll certainly slip back into them again, tonight they've been sloughing off, and now we hold each other, empty and naked as the light changes above us.

It's something like praise. Whisper choruses sounding behind me, insinuating themselves when I least expect, whispers of occasional comforts and graces reminding me what is true. A thankfulness I feel watching Abby tiptoe forward into the lapping waves, arms pinwheeling, then reel back, breathless.

Dancing with Alex beneath the stoplight like something from a Fred Astaire movie, right hands clasped and held aloft, left at our waists, dancing to a melody we're inventing or remembering, one eye on the street for traffic, our bodies don't feel like bodies at all, but like an alien music bound to earth only by our breath, like a huge spreading flower swaying on the spindle of a stem.

A lone early morning runner jogs up Elm. Seeing us, he spins still jogging, a full turn, applauding silently before continuing on.

I love Alex because I see him, see him clearly, perfectly, for an instant. And, having seen him, how can I not love him. How can this seeing not shake me, not take my breath, leave a soft scar of intimacy. It's strong, rampant, directionless. How can there ever be too much love in the world.

That night, at the corner of Washington and Elm, it's a place he inhabits in me. As if love isn't a feeling but a location as physical as the street itself. A location that can only be shared. A place to stand.

The adoration I feel listening to my daughters sleep, the warm scent of their skin and hair. It comes over me without cause, in the passing contact with a stranger on the street or the sudden presence of Alex or the private whispers of a couple at the next table, as a swell and a catch in the throat. All the words I used with Alex that night to try to define my place within the burn and sway of the world, all the words that tumbled out of me, undisguised. It's something I claimed, for the first time, that night.

I open my eyes. Caleb's features are soft in the glow of the dashboard lights. Gray trees spin by the window and the waves of the road are more pronounced now, gradual hills rising and falling. His hair is tossed by the breeze, and he needs a shave. He's humming softly to a tune on the radio, fingers spidering along the top of the steering wheel, humming the way he did in the moments after Meghan's birth.

He stands by the bed, Meghan bundled in his arms, her eyes wide before him. He sways with her side to side. Before the birth, his terror with the thought of a child had been palpable, leaking through as a tightness in his voice, a panicked glance. But in this moment, this first moment, he vanishes into her. As if her gaze takes him in so completely that he disappears for an instant, his expression silent and awed. I can see the room around him has faded, even I have faded for a moment. It's just he and Meghan locked into something so powerful that he loses all thought and all pretense. He's absolutely beautiful.

In a moment he begins to sway gently, side to side, while the nurse busies herself with my pulse and the CNA gathers the bedding and I let my head fall back for an instant to the pillow. He begins to hum, to sing to her. A spontaneous tune. He doesn't know he's singing; he doesn't even know he's breathing.

So many private things pass between them. A language is there I cannot enter. In that instant they know each other absolutely. It's a wordless and constant knowing, completely their own. It is impossible. How can there ever be too much love in the world.

Abby is muttering in her sleep, thick liquid sentences. Or perhaps she's sharing a story with Meghan, her head slumped left in the car seat, her hands folded in her lap. Meghan rustles, shifting position, licking her lips.

One day I'll tell Caleb about Alex. I'll find the words to share the tenderness with him. I don't doubt he'll understand. I imagine the curious spark in his eye, a curl of a smile as he listens. But not tonight, with the glow upon me; not tonight, my skin tingling with Alex's touch. Tonight, there are no words.

I open my eyes. Knowing the car, knowing the wheels beneath me. Opening my eyes to a dark and foreign road before me. The hiss of the tires, the featureless night. I open my eyes to place myself. In the car beside Caleb.

"Hey there," he says, noticing me stir. "What's up?"

I stifle a yawn. "Nothing," I say. I wind away from the seat, uncurling, pressing my bare toes into the floor of the car until my legs are fully extended.

Caleb arches an eyebrow in mock surprise. "Nothing?"

I take his hand from where it's dropped to his thigh, twining my fingers into his. "Not a thing."

He glances over and smiles. I rub my eyes with my loose hand, turning in the seat, my back to the door to study his face. In the glow of the dashboard lights with the gray trees streaking by the window.

The smile has settled into his face. I can feel it trickle into his fingers. He glances over again. We'll be home soon.

TINY, IMPOSSIBLE

The world is flat. Until it isn't. That's what I think. On the train you have your own thoughts and you let them flow around you. You avoid eye contact because you never know what you might see and how the responsibility might mark you.

You know the tunnel lights are blinking past the windows. You feel the bodies swaying in concert with each incline and curve, you hear the murmur of conversations, the wet shuffling of feet, the sniffling of the baby in the stroller. You stare at your phone though there's really nothing to see.

They pretend you aren't there. You pretend. It's a tacit agreement broken only by an announcement, a delay, the train grinding to a halt in the darkness between stations. They all have their own lives. They have their own phones. They're all staring down at them.

Your body knows the others are there. It adjusts to proximity, shifts balance in the accelerations. Your body knows they're there, but your mind has lost them. You draw your thoughts around you. It doesn't matter what they are. They hold the world away.

You hold to the rail by the door, tilting to the side when it slides open, then returning to place. As the car fills, you make yourself smaller, press into the rail. You look at your feet or your phone. As the car fills it gets louder but it's indeterminate. It would take an effort to follow a conversation unless it's taking place right at my ear.

The train is a shifting border between waking and dreaming, between one station and another. Some people nod off, their heads lolling with the rhythm of the tracks. The best can sleep soundly yet never miss their stop.

The train fills and you can notice it without retaining any detail; you'd never be able to describe anyone near you clearly, you'd be a useless police witness. The recorded announcements. The hiss of the doors opening and closing. The braking and acceleration. It all occurs at the edge of your awareness.

You bump into your body, into your limbs. That's what happens, I bump into my body all at once. I drop into it with a thump. My center of gravity lowers, my legs brace, my fingers tighten on the pole and the world takes shape around me.

My eyes move from the floor. I bring my hand up from my side, my hand with the phone. But I don't look at the phone. I look at you. I don't know how long I look at you. It's hard to say. But there's something that holds my eyes there.

And you look up. Our eyes meet. We don't turn away. We simply look at each other. As if we recognize each other. And maybe we do.

— You were there.
— I'd seen you before. On the train.
— You were there and I'd seen you before.
— I'd seen you. I didn't know you.
— I knew you were on the train. Sometimes.
— What was it?
— What was what.
— What made you see me.

— It was the scarf.

— The scarf.

— The red scarf with flecks of gold. It was the scarf.

— The scarf.

— No, not the scarf. It was your hand, open on your thigh.

— My hand.

— You were sitting. Reading.

— You were standing.

— I was standing. Near the door.

— Your hand was on the rail.

— My hand was on the rail. My backpack was on my shoulder.

— The blue one. With all the zippers.

— The blue one. You held your book open in one hand.

— *The Savage Detectives*.

— *The Savage Detectives*. The book was in one hand.

— I love that book.

— Me too. Your other hand was open on your thigh.

— My other hand.

— It was open. I was standing by the rail. Watching your hand.

— My hand.

— It was your hand I saw first. That was the first thing.

— Then the scarf?

— Then the scarf.

— Then?

— Then?

— Then.

— I guess it was your eyes.

— My eyes?

— Your eyes. But not really.

— What then.

— After your hand. And the scarf.

— After the scarf.

— After the scarf you just bloomed. You were there all at once.

— I was there.
— All at once. You were there. To me, I mean.
— I see.
— It's like those science films.
— Which ones?
— The ones where you see the seed break the ground then bloom into a plant all in five seconds, the ones where the whole process happens right before your eyes.
— I was a sprout.
— You were a sprout. And then you weren't.

I'm awake all at once, like a cartoon character whose eyes are twice the size of their body. I don't awaken with a start. I don't jump. There is no adrenaline rush. My eyes simply open and I'm awake. My body takes longer.

The sunlight slants through the blinds, burning hard parallel lines onto the blanket at the foot of the bed. The white walls glow a bit. I rustle slightly, rubbing my feet together beneath the sheet but I don't want to wake you. I want to lie beside you for a moment as I compose myself. My feet, my hands, flicker to life. I can feel my back at the mattress, my body slowly discovering its weight and reach, the awareness rising in me, seeping into my arms and legs.

I'm running to the station. The cool air, the buildings streaking by, the pages ruffling in my hand. You'd forgotten your music and I had to run it to you before the train came. It's only been a few weeks, but I've still had to run your music to the station twice. You kiss me when I hand it over, just in time, and you board the train, pushing the sheets into your case.

I watch you. I'm shameless when I watch you, so sometimes you notice. I watch you. I don't know what you're doing but I know you're doing it. Washing a dish, stopping to pet a dog, dropping your tea bag into a cup.

I like watching you. The way you spread everything

out on the floor before you leave for a performance. The violin and bow, the rosin. The cloth and the shoulder rest. That lotion you use after because your hands get dry. And your music.

You sit cross-legged before it all, your eyes flickering over each thing, then you begin to slowly pack it away. There's such a quietness to you, but it's like a million tiny gears turning together, it's that kind of quiet.

You'd been practicing that one sonata, so it was on the stand in the corner and you'd left it, so I had to run it to you. I didn't mind. I liked it, really. I liked watching you get on the train. Liked watching the train pull away with you in the window. I walked back slowly, stopped for a coffee, and sat on the bench at the corner to drink it.

You're not awake yet. I listen to your breathing as my body assembles itself. I'm filling with a clear liquid or a dusty, amber light. I turn toward your bare back. I flatten my palm between your shoulder blades. I close my eyes.

I don't know, I must have been seven or eight, I think, and I suddenly realized how much of the world I was missing. Maybe something like this happened to you. I mean, all at once I realized how much I physically just could not see. And I don't mean in Trinidad or Nepal. I mean in my own yard, my own house, just how much of the world there was. At first it was a crushing blow, it made my head hurt, my eyes ache. I'd never know what the dog did while I was at school, I'd never see the labyrinths of tunnel the ants were constructing under the backyard, I'd never know what my mom and dad talked about before bed. There were all these things I would never see.

This wanting to see, it was obsessive, voracious. I felt it all the time hot along my skin like a fever. There was so much world and so little me. I wanted to be everywhere at once, a fly on the wall in every room on earth. There was a secret there and I knew it.

I'd be watching TV in the living room, at the same time listening to my mother's phone conversation in the kitchen. I'd hear the pots bubbling on the stove and the dog barking three doors down and the sound of a lawnmower the next street over and I'd try to put the picture together in my mind, of all these things happening at once, I'd try to imagine myself floating above it and the sounds would help me. I was still there. I was in the scene. In my living room, watching TV and enjoying it. I could see myself sitting there, I could feel myself laugh at the next joke. My body, cross-legged on the floor before the TV, that's what pinned me to earth.

I'd lie in the damp grass at night. I'd spread my arms and legs. I was making myself bigger. Instead of simply widening my eyes, I was widening my whole body. I could feel the world along my skin, filling my ears, my nose, my mouth, I could feel the world pressing into me from all sides. My body was a sail and I wanted to catch as much wind as possible.

The sky was black, the stars were burning. The grass was damp and all of the night was humming. The world was firm beneath me. I was sure I could feel the spin of the planets.

Everything was bright and fierce. I was bright and fierce. And all I wanted was to see with my whole body. I wanted to see everything. I wanted it all at once.

I don't turn on the lights. I just let myself in and put my case and my bag on the sofa, unwind my scarf, take off my coat. Then I stand in the living room for a moment. In the dark. The apartment smells of coffee and spice, something dark and red. My arms are still tingling; I let them fall to my sides, loosening my fingers.

It's quiet. I can hear the traffic from the street and a lonely dog barking, but the other sounds are buttery and light. They have a softness that makes the room warm and inviting. I slip off each shoe with the heel of my foot and curl my toes on the hardwood floor.

I don't remember the train home or the moments before I played. I know I talked and smiled and swayed through the world. I know there were conversations and jokes. I know there was wine after and those around me were laughing. I was laughing. I don't remember climbing the stairs or walking onstage.

I remember the spin of the music, the way it tore from the instrument and enveloped me. The tiny impossible surface of the bow at the strings. The tiny, impossible notes on the page. The sense of never being alive before that moment, of not remembering what being alive was until that moment then remembering it all at once and it wasn't memory then, it was just being. The music, my fingertips on the violin and bow, my breath. The sound, the feeling; there was no difference.

There's more light in the bedroom. The streetlight throws shadows, parallel lines along the ceiling above the bed.

Today was a holiday and you were home all day. You in one room and me in the other. My practicing didn't bother you because my practicing never bothers you and now and then you ask me about a phrase or a melody. I'm practicing and you're in your chair. Your chair, with the lamp and the table beside it.

You, with your neat stacks of papers on the table by the chair and the way you take one up and smooth it in your lap then read, marking as you go. When you're finished, you glance through one more time, occasionally catching something new, then you drop the paper to the stack on the floor beside you.

In the bedroom, I stand by the bed. I let my clothes fall around me to the floor. It feels good to be naked, to feel the air along my bare skin. It's cool and goosebumps rise on my arms. You're already asleep.

There's the moment the orchestra rises in the first tuned chord. There's no music yet, but everyone is present, sharing the same note. The thrill of that chord rides low in my body between my anchored legs, pulsing outward. From that one note, anything can happen.

Our note is not quite a silence. I wait to find it. I pull back the blanket and the sheet. I can feel the warmth you've held rising from the bed. I lie down and hollow into you.

My arms and legs release their weight first. The day begins to lose its hold. The distance grows as events fold into memory. You in your chair. Glancing into the darkness of the hall beyond the bright lights. The first strike of the bow upon the strings. My body becomes an empty space held in place by the warmth radiating from yours.

It's dark and it's quiet and any thoughts bleed away but they leave the music behind. It's soft, constant, like whispers just at the tips of my fingers.

The world always seemed big, too big. I felt small at that age and sometimes that smallness frightened me but other times it was a comfort. It seemed like I had to choose, to choose what to know.

I wanted to know one thing, just one thing. I thought if I knew music, if I just concentrated and studied and practiced and really knew music, then that would be my anchor. But music just kept getting deeper and wider, deeper and wider, and I realized there was no knowing to it. It just was. It just is.

It's like a mountain stream. I can fish, kayak, I can swim in it. I can sit on the bank and listen as it flows by. It will always be what it is. It's me that's changing.

The thing about knowing is, as soon as I know, I stop seeing. As soon as I knew where everything was in your kitchen, I didn't have to see it anymore. I stopped seeing it. The kitchen became featureless. As soon as I knew where you put the spices, which cabinet held the saucepans, I didn't have to notice. As soon as I knew you slept on the left side of the bed, I slipped into the right.

The trick is not to know. To keep on not knowing. It's not so hard once you realize your knowing is mostly a story, just a bunch of stories you tell yourself. So much knowing is like that.

I don't know you. I know I don't know you. There's something in you I know, but it shifts and changes shape. You're always changing shape.

Last Sunday, I was at the table in the cafe and you were getting our coffees and I was watching a tree nodding in the breeze, just watching a tree, and I looked over as you turned from the counter with the cups in your hand and you seemed a completely different person. There was a shock, a thrill.

The trick when I pick up the violin is not to know how to play it, then to play it. To look at the sheet music for the "Sonata in A-major" and have no idea how the sounds fit together, then to listen. Knowing is this story I tell myself that tries to keep the world from changing but the world changes anyway.

I had my book, I was reading, I was in my own world. There were moments when I didn't know where I was. Remembering it now, I can feel myself flickering like a flame. That day. On the train.

I felt you before I saw you. It was a tug that came out of nowhere as if my name had been whispered. Do you know that feeling? Of thinking you've heard your name spoken on the street or in a room and you turn and there's no one there?

That day. On the train. I felt you before I saw you. Otherwise, I never would have looked.

The world is flat. Until it isn't.

Arturo and Ulises are drinking, they're always drinking, they drink a lot, and they're plotting to find their poetic hero. They talk about women, about drinking, about poetry. Mostly about poetry. Visceral Realism. The glasses are dirty, the bottle is nearly empty, the floors are dirty, the music is loud, and it's 3 a.m. so there aren't a lot of other people around. I know once they attempt to stand, they'll sway, their hands clutching at the table to steady themselves. I know once they reach the street they'll simply wander away in opposite directions without a word. But now, I'm listening. I don't know if they're making sense, but I like listening to their conversation and, strangely, I like them.

The flatness of the page opens up and I'm surrounded. It happens with the music; when I'm playing, I can feel I'm disappearing, but it's not disappearing really. Maybe it's the opposite of that. There's no separation. It's hard to explain.

There was a particular passage I liked. I think I went back and marked it. I remember the train rocking, I was held in place by the people on both sides. The train was rocking and Arturo and Ulises were drinking and there was this passage that, well, it wasn't necessarily beautiful, but it was perfect. It was just perfect, too perfect to read on. I had to stop for a moment and let the book fall closed between my thumb, I had to close my eyes. I knew so much then. I don't know what I knew but I knew it.

I'm not sure how many stops we'd made. The train had filled. We'd crossed the bridge. There were people nestled in beside me in their puffy coats. The man to my right was snoring softly and the woman to my left smelled of jasmine and I was holding a space open for Arturo and Ulises.

The feeling is whole, then it breaks into parts. It breaks into parts so I can talk about it. It was like someone had called my name. I looked around the train and everyone was in their own world. No one was in mine. I looked around the train.

You were looking at me. I caught your glance. And I didn't look away, as if we recognized each other. And maybe we did.

— You were waiting.
— I wasn't waiting.
— You were waiting for me.
— Not for you.
— Someone then. You were waiting for someone.

— I wasn't waiting.
— You were.
— I wasn't waiting for someone.
— What were you waiting for?
— Some thing.
— A thing.
— A gesture, I don't know.
— A kind of thing?
— A gesture, a collision.
— A collision?
— Like colors striking, or light and dark. I don't know.
— You don't know.
— I don't know how to say it.
— You don't know.
— How to say it.
— You were waiting.
— I was waiting.
— Ah. . .
— But I'm always waiting. Aren't you.
— Waiting?
— Aren't you always waiting. Some part of you
    anticipating something.
— Something, like what.
— Some part of you wanting to be sure. To feel,
    something.
— Like what.
— Like anything. Something, anything.
— You were waiting.
— I was waiting. But not for someone.
— Not for someone.
— Or something.
— For me, were you waiting for me?
— I wasn't waiting for you.
— No.
— I was waiting for myself to arrive.

DEVASTATION TOUR

My mother was not a Mennonite, by any means, but they often enlisted her to work for Mennonite Disaster Services because she could get shit done. My mother, for her part, would only take short term assignments with NGOs. She liked to say she wanted to be responsive; to be free to move between organizations from crisis to crisis. In this way, she could choose where we went next.

The Mennonites not only accepted her, they embraced her, especially in large scale disasters. Hurricanes, floods, earthquakes; when there were a number of cogs that had to mesh and turn. She was a master at driving, coaxing, or shaming people into doing what she wanted, and the Mennonites knew it.

She'd allow them their moments of prayer, their mild proselytizing to the afflicted; she'd even allow their sometimes-stilted language and the occasional quote from the Bible; but when it was time to work, it was time to work. You put the Bible down and picked up the handsaw or the hammer. That's why you were there.

I know they sometimes puzzled over her. I wondered

if they called her a bitch under their breath. Suppliers, staff at Home Depot, the heads of other nonprofits did, I'm sure. I'd heard them more than once. I don't think the Mennonites knew the word except in relation to breeding. Besides, they had the expectation of a hard life. They saw it as a gift from God. Who were they to question the form their tribulations came in?

Much about my mother was a secret even to me. I heard about her life in snatches on the planes or in the busses we took between disasters. She didn't like to talk about herself but the occasional fact slipped out.

She'd always relate events in an offhand way, as if listing flight delays from an arrival and departure board. Her story was an abandoned jigsaw puzzle, so loosely assembled I couldn't discern the image.

"Found Jesus my first year of college, lost him soon after; too much whimpering and smiling went along with him. All these grown white people whining about their life then smiling just enough in this manufactured joy to get you to listen to more of their whimpering. I couldn't deal with the Jesus."

I'd nod, the way I usually did. Sometimes I'd ask questions and she was almost always good about answering, but sometimes I couldn't think of any. I'd just nod and return to my book. My mother kept me in books; she was perfect that way.

She took me with her everywhere and told people I was being home-schooled but, really, she simply bought me any book I wanted. If she was working a soup line I was beside her; if she was jerking wet drywall from the frame of a house I was there, standing in the shin deep mud slime, surrounded by blooms of black mold. She didn't believe in protecting children.

"The world is what it is and it ain't nothing else. We got to stand up to it." She didn't believe there was any protection to be had.

John Yoder met us at the airport, forty miles outside the flooding. It was still raining further south near the delta—twenty-three inches in eighteen hours—and nearer airports were closed. John was tall, lean, with sandy hair raked across his forehead, a full beard and mustache. His shoulders were square, his eyes a bright blue, and for years I thought he and my mother should get married. When I was younger, I liked to imagine climbing into his lap at night and pressing him to read to me. Or his scratchy beard leaning down to kiss me on the forehead before bed. Now, I was ten. I'd given up on that plan and hadn't come up with a replacement.

John embraced my mother before she could stop him, partially, I believe, because he knew the attention made her uncomfortable. My mother's arms flapped at her sides, her shoulders rising, her palms turned upward. John Yoder chuckled. "Constance, God bless you for coming. It's so good to see you."

Without waiting for a response, he turned to hug me. "Abigail, you're growing up so fast." He winked. It always made me smile when he winked.

I sat in the truck in the middle as we drove South, John Yoder briefing my mother on the situation, my mother asking questions, something in me finding a quiet and still hollow between them. She and I always seemed to be a blur in motion, never exactly where we were, always moving instead toward the next thing. So, it was nice to feel John's body on one side and hers on the other, to feel held in place for a moment.

John Yoder asked me about our travels and the books I'd been reading but my mother was ready to get down to business. She wanted the updated forecast for the next few days. She wanted to know which services were in place, what materials were in route. She wanted to go out in the boats tomorrow morning.

"You're going to need as many people as you can get."

He nodded. "The North Part of town. It'll take the Guard a while to get there. Water'll be worse, houses will be shakier."

I was wilting, whether from the narcotic effect of the

airport or a sense of anticipation for the coming days. In times like these, we slept where and when we could. My mother often worked eighteen to twenty hours a day at the height of a disaster. When I was younger, I'd find a place to curl up and someone would toss a blanket or a coat over me.

Waking up, I'd have to go looking for her. She would have moved to the next tent or the next house. Now, I just worked beside her. I knew to rest when I could.

The conversation unfolded around me as I drifted in and out of sleep. At first it was all practicality. What happened tomorrow my mother called the devastation tour. The idea was to assess the damage and begin to decide what could and could not be saved. I'd heard this conversation many times and the details weren't all that interesting, so I dozed, my head falling to John Yoder's shoulder.

Later in the drive, their voices had lowered to a range of skeptical intimacy that seemed to pull me from a dream.

"What is it you want, Constance?"

"You should know that by now, John Yoder."

John Yoder wasn't present at every storm and flood MDS handled. I think he worked the Southern States. But, whenever we saw him, there were conversations like this, often into the night. It was a way of talking that never seemed to conclude, merely pause, in the weeks or months between.

"Maybe I do. Maybe I just want to hear you say it."

Constance sighed. It wasn't the sigh I got when I wanted to go to a movie or buy a new CD. It was a patient sigh, with a little bit of care present as an undertone.

"I want to burn all the ego out of me," she tells him.

He is silent for a moment.

"The Lord doesn't want you to burn, Constance."

"Makes no difference what The Lord wants, John Yoder," my mother's voice nearly as soft as his. "No difference at all."

My mother inhales—an inhalation replacing a sigh—then straightens herself in the seat beside me. My eyes are closed but I know she's staring directly out the windshield before her into the opening night.

"I'm not going to talk about your faith, John Yoder, because you know me and you know I think your faith is for shit. Not just yours, mind you. Anybody's."

I have to assume he talked about these things with my mother precisely because she didn't care and that my mother talked to him because she knew there was no way to offend him. It was a connection that had nothing to do with words or belief and this must have been somehow liberating for them both.

Soon, rain began to pound the windshield and I could hear the larger puddles sweep up around the doors of the truck, as if we were already in tomorrow's boats, the water swirling around us. John Yoder held the truck steady through the standing water and I dozed, imagining myself riding a bubble just above the surface of the water channeling into gutters and downspouts. Soon, I was asleep for good.

I wouldn't remember him carrying me into the motel and lowering me to the bed, his scratchy beard at my cheek. I wouldn't remember Constance turning out the light and she and John Yoder standing in the open door to the street talking into the night. But, knowing that it happened was the closest I ever got to a feeling of home.

The connection is bad, of course; it always is. So, it takes patience to have a conversation. We try to accept the delays, the fading signals, the sentences we have to repeat. My mother is not known for her patience, but she's trying. She's in some river village in Venezuela while I'm pacing a hotel room in Khartoum.

She'd been talking about dysentery and alcohol wipes. I'd been talking about the drought. This is how it goes between us.

Nearing sixty, the work she does isn't as dangerous

as before. It's mostly clinic setups for WHO and supply lines for vaccination programs, though now and then I hear she's in a refugee camp somewhere in Pakistan or Turkey. She still doesn't have a mailing address.

By now, she's sort of an NGO legend, having lost none of her ability to cajole and blackmail over the years. Often, at conferences, I'm called upon to smile blankly as someone relates still another story about Constance and her unique gifts. To which I reply, because it's true: "I don't know anyone who's saved more actual lives than my mother."

"Goddamn drug companies and the government scalping every cent," she's telling me, as if I didn't know, as if I'd never heard this before. "Think of what we could get done if we didn't have to deal with assholes."

The Sudanese night outside my window is spread black, stars above and city below. It's a dark river studded with the pulsing colors of buoys and boats. Everything wavers; the air is in motion with the heat which just adds to the liquid illusion. I watch the shimmer as my mother talks about paying off the Governor, the local officials, the truck drivers, about paying twice as much as she should for a boat and motor, then paying three times the going price for gasoline.

"If a gun had been handy, I could've just shot them. Saved myself the expense."

She comes to visit Max and me once or twice a year in Silver Spring, but she really just comes to see Sadie. She's completely comfortable rolling on the floor with the dog or tossing a ball in the backyard but when Sadie is finally exhausted and collapses into her bed, my mother is at sea. She paces the room, scratches at her skin as if allergic to clean clothes. It's never more than a day or two before some new crisis sweeps her away again.

My mother sways into another conversational lane. She's ready to talk about me now.

She asks about Max and the dog, but these are

really just her opening moves. There is no doubt where she is going.

"I understand you not wanting to get dirty. It's the *New Yorker* article that bothers me, those fluffy *HuffPost* pieces that make you out as some kind of Celebrity of Misery."

The line crackles with stray electricity. My suitcase is open on one of the beds, files spread across the desk and the dresser, on top of the television. I plant my feet before the window and take a deep breath.

"I know it must feel good," my mother says, "but, I mean, once you start believing that shit, how do you ever know you're doing any good?"

Any pause is an admission of guilt.

"I don't believe it but it gets the word out. People begin to understand the struggles here. Congressmen begin to take notice. Sudan becomes part of the global conversation. Besides, Constance, how do we ever know we're doing any good?'

"Well, I see the people who survive," she parries. "They're here in the next room."

I know this isn't an attack, that she's simply trying to make a point. It's a question she needles me with when she can because she's needled herself with it her entire life. I also know she won't accept any answer I offer.

I could tell her the job gives me the semblance of a normal life. I only travel a couple of weeks a year, the rest I can spend with Max and Sadie. But it's the guilt of comfort she's holding over me; it's the way a lifestyle fundamentally betrays the people we try to help.

Constance apologizes after a few minutes in the muttering, nebulous way she always apologizes, as if wrestling with an impenetrable ritual newly discovered and barely understood. She asks again about Max and Sadie, forgetting she had already, but I can tell she's depleted the resources she reserves for personal conversation. I can tell she's planning her day tomorrow as the words lose force.

I float above the city and the night. Though I have a beautiful view, the glass and the height protect me from the particulars of the Sudanese streets. I can rest safely above them. Even the noise of the traffic becomes a slight ambient tone barely audible beneath the hum of the air conditioning.

Maybe one day, we'll have mundane conversations about gardens, heirloom tomatoes, and hummingbird feeders, she and I. Maybe, we'll rock together on a wide porch overlooking a freshly mown field. With cups of tea. Maybe we'll have tea.

But for now her identity, and mine, require catastrophe.

The boats smell. The volunteers smell. The water smells worse; brown water like a sewer mixed with mud and stirred with branches, weeds, plastic bags, garbage. And bodies. Dogs float by. A bloated deer. John Yoder turns the boat away from the corpse of a man in red shorts, his blue t-shirt twisted around his frame, beached in a field of mud that was once a front yard, then discretely radios back to report it.

The smell is a mix of sweat, damp clothes, mud and shit. It's too soon for rot, but in another day or so, as the water recedes, more corpses will be stranded and the stench of death and mold will become overpowering. The water itself protects us from that now.

It's 8 a.m. and already hot. Our clothes cling to our skin in the thick humidity and sweat runs down my sides. I'm sitting on a thin aluminum bench in the center of the boat, John Yoder behind steering with the motor, my mother at the bow. After the chaos of the staging area, where someone is always wailing, the water has its peace. There's the kind of reassurance in the force of nature and the way it puts us in our place.

Strangely, the smell of rot always has this cleanness nested within it for me; it's the quiet emptiness I can feel after vomiting, or when a fever begins to subside. A kind of surrendered emptiness that I can't imagine until it's somehow wrenched from me. It's a momentary pause in which new things can happen. The possibility of something else.

We are always working in the poorer parts of every town. MDS looks for the houses where the residents might not have the money to fix the roofs, mend the porches, replace the windows; the whole point is to help those in the most need. The Mennonites are good that way; quietly marching into areas others might avoid.

The houses are often small, old, and in need of much repair even before a storm, so that sometimes the rising water tears them from their roots and they simply float away whole, or they buckle at a crumbling foundation losing one wall at a time until they collapse on themselves.

The boats ahead are collecting people, from second- or third-story windows, from their roofs, people who have been standing knee deep in water since yesterday in the second floor of their house, people who have pushed family albums, quilts and keepsakes onto their roof through a hole they chopped with an axe kept there for the purpose. One boat holds an elderly woman wrapped in a blanket and shawl sitting in a wheelchair and I have to wonder where they collected her and how they maneuvered both her and the wheelchair into the boat. She looks regal, though, like a queen transported in her palanquin. Helicopters buzz by overhead but, for now, they're en route to the south side of town where the money is.

There's almost no visible current on the surface of the water but we can sometimes hear the submerged cars shift or a house shuddering as we pass. In water like this, the situation can change in a moment.

My mother pushes large branches, floating barrels, and other refuse from the front of the boat as John Yoder steers among the trash. They're quiet with each other now, and I'm quiet too. Yet, now and then at intervals, we call out loudly to the water and the empty houses and the tops of trees, "Hello! Anyone here?!" Just in case someone has fallen asleep or is away from a window.

John Yoder's voice sounds first, low and booming, then my mother's, then I chirp in. I like to believe that it's my voice any children will hear, as if the adults are pitched at too low a frequency. I like to imagine a young girl waking to my call in the darkness then shouting back to me in a language only I can hear. I would give John Yoder directions; he would be confused at first, but he would trust me.

He had promised me pancakes for dinner and I could taste them already, light with a thin brown crust soaked in maple syrup. Maybe I'd even get sausage. Links, not patties.

The boat continues in the rank water, past the submerged roofs of cars and second floors of houses, their windows broken and empty. We see the boats ahead of us picking up the stranded then turning back to deliver them to the staging area. Eventually, we become the lead boat.

Turning the corner around a stand of trees, we find a partially submerged house with movement on the roof. As we approach we can make out two figures, both standing, waving their arms in wide arcs above their heads.

"We're coming!" John Yoder booms.

It's a girl, younger than me and a woman who must be her grandmother. The girl wears a blue and white patterned dress with a white collar, her spindly limbs splaying out at all angles. Her grandmother is heavier, her stocky legs planted in broad, black shoes. There are stains on her dress where it has been wet and dried numerous times. There's a raw hole in the roof where they escaped, the shingles pushed up like jagged black teeth around it.

As we approach, we can see the Grandmother is breathing heavily, hands on her knees. She stares down at the roof for a moment, attempting to catch her breath, then returns her gaze to our boat for reassurance.

My mother speaks calmly as the boat nears, repeating her name and asking theirs, attempting to normalize the situation as much as she can so they don't panic when the boat arrives. She asks them if they're hurt and they say no. She asks if there's anyone else in the house and they say no. She asks them to sit and they do.

The grandmother is crying now in relief, large tears rolling down her cheeks as she clutches her granddaughter, whose name is Tasha. I'm talking to Tasha, my mother is talking to Linda, when John Yoder draws the boat alongside the roofline.

My mother takes Linda's hand, easing her toward the rim of the roof and the side of the boat. Linda's other hand slides from around Tasha's side as she stands, lowering one foot then the other into the boat and, suddenly alone, Tasha becomes too terrified to move. She's trembling, staring before her into the dirty water, her eyes wide and unblinking.

I don't really think about it. I step onto the roof and sit down beside her. I don't know what I'm saying to her; I'm just trying to tell her everything will be alright. I can hear my mother soothing the grandmother in the boat. At some point, Constance steps onto the roof.

I offer Tasha my hand and she rakes her wrist across her face at her tears, then takes it. Her fingers are bony and cool. We stand up slowly, balancing against the slant of the roof. We're about to turn toward the boat when the house shudders and shifts. We stumble backward, tripping over the upraised shingles, tumbling into the open hole in the roof and the water beneath and I lose her hand in the fall.

The water is cold and I gasp, coming up for air, my arms thrashing against the attic roof. I can see the sunlight through the jagged hole. The water churns around me in the sudden darkness. It's carrying me back into the attic and I struggle against it.

Constance's hand reaches down from the hole in the roof, she must be kneeling or lying on her stomach.

Her hand comes down and snatches Tasha, first by the dress, then by the arm, hoisting her up into the sunlight.

The house shifts and drops, pulling at its moorings. I go under again, the dirty curtain folding over me. There are leaves sticking to my mouth and it hurts when I gulp in water, some space in my chest filling with darkness. I can see the hole in the roof from beneath the skin of the surface and I struggle to get there but it's suddenly so much further away.

Something falls on my head and I go under again. When I open my eyes Constance is there, still clutching the other girl, both of them staring at me, eyes wide with horror, and John Yoder, soaked to the skin, is pressing hard at my chest. I turn my head and the dirty brown water pours out. My mouth is left with grass and grit until I vomit again.

For years, I couldn't really remember what happened that day; it was a long, bright blur that ended back at the staging area by an ambulance in John Yoder's arms. That was all I could remember, resting in his arms. Then the dreams began and the memories returned slowly, one shard at a time, sharp things that worked themselves to the surface of my skin from deep inside.

So, I was never completely sure of everything that happened, never felt I could trust my memory. And, I never knew for certain whether God had spared me through grace or spite.

Six months later, I was sent away to boarding school where there were clean sheets and hot meals and girls who talked about Nirvana and had never read a single book straight through. I learned, over the years, to wear a dress, giggle, and do quadratic equations. I went home with friends for weekends to houses with compounds larger than many of the villages I had lived in.

I became the kind of student who was accepted to NYU and, once accepted, the kind of student to go. I never stopped feeling I'd somehow failed my mother.

Or God. Or both. In the dank alleyways of my soul, perhaps there is no difference between the two.

Eventually, I abandoned God completely, feeling no loss. It was unceremonious; accomplished with a shrug. My loss was deeper, something not quite an emptiness. It had no particular center in my body. It simply permeated every cell, leaving me with an absence. That absence was an active, gnawing thing.

And because I've always been haunted by John Yoder's simple faith, the absence is difficult to accept. His faith itself I can rationalize away, but not the way it haunts me. It awakens an organ deep inside my body that longs for surrender. Total abandonment.

It brings about a specific hunger. It's impossible to say whether the hunger itself, or the inability to be filled, is the remnant of my mother. So, even after a Masters in Psychology, I found myself back at one NGO after another. Nothing else could promise even the possibility of satisfying the hunger.

I know my mother has saved many lives. I know I have, too. I can't stop asking myself what those lives were saved for. The saved are forgotten the next day. The saved continue to struggle in appalling conditions. The saved live in a country where the same thing will happen again in two years, five years.

My line of sight is filled by the grim immensity of need. I believe I'm doing good; I just don't have faith that it's true. And what is there in the absence of faith? Doubt. Only doubt. And the same questions, again and again.

I realize I've been standing before the window for a long time and the phone is still in my hand. Some of the shops below have closed, so there are fewer lights now and the heat has abated just enough that the landscape has stabilized, losing its liquid shimmer. I press my free hand against the glass, hoping to feel the warmth of the night outside but the air conditioning has taken care of that. The glass is hard and cool.

The phone line is dead, of course. As so often happens with these calls, eventually the connection just drops out. There are no goodbyes, no plans for the next rendezvous, the conversation simply ends. We don't attempt to re-establish the connection.

I slip the phone into my pocket, wishing there were a window I could open, wondering if I should take the elevator down to the street and walk in the heavy night air. I know what the State Department would say about that.

When I was young I believed the Mennonites talked to their God, possibly in a secret language only they could claim. They seemed peaceful and confident. They seemed unwavering.

John Yoder, tossing lumber into a truck or wiping away sweat and sawdust by a spreading tree: he'd look around himself at all the work going on. He'd be anchored and peaceful and he'd allow himself to relish that peace for a moment before returning to work.

His self was never in the way. It never occurred to him he could do anything else. Helping was natural, nearly genetic; not a thing he had to think about. And because there were no motives, he never had to question them.

God was hard for the Mennonites—a demanding absentee landlord due back any minute—but He was harder for my mother. Apparently, mother had one raging argument with Him, then they vowed never to speak again. Ever after, they stood like angry five-year-olds at opposite ends of the playground, backs to each other.

My mother denied God's existence in a way that made Him ubiquitous. I deny my mother much the same way. The irony doesn't escape me.

We rely on the storms, she and I, the earthquakes and mudslides, to give our life purpose. We thrive on the need and curse it at the same time. The need supplants our private desires. The need allows us to believe we matter. In the clearest moments, the need overwhelms us and all that is left is action. When the personal rears its ugly head and it's not the storm we want, we simply choose another.

I turn to the suitcase on the bed and for an instant I don't remember whether I'm packing or unpacking. My clothes look like they belong to another person; I can't imagine anyone actually wearing them. The files spread on the comforter must have been left by the last occupant.

Eventually I find myself again, where I am and what I'm doing here: the dress for the reception tomorrow night, the program outline for the Interior Minister, the number for my contact at *The Times*. I decide I should be unpacking and that's what I do.

I want to know what to hold on to and what to give up. I want to be back home in Silver Spring, not half a world away. I want to be climbing into a crisp bed beside a sleeping Max and I want him to roll toward me, still asleep, slip his arm around my waist and hold me until sleep takes me. I want just one of those unpredictable, random moments when I completely forget myself.

What I feel is small, blue, and hard. What I feel is something less than an emptiness.

One day, my mother will be old and alone and our story will still be raw, unexamined. She was trying to burn her self away and I, as an extension of that self, was simply collateral damage. I want to think I'll be there for her when she needs me. But maybe, when the time comes, I'll reach for someone else.

The next day we're back in the boats. My mother wouldn't hear of John Yoder's protestations that I should, perhaps, stay at the motel and simply rest, watch TV for the day. There was work to be done and we were going to do it.

Everyone is concerned about me. Everyone is impressed with how strong and fearless I am. They congratulate my mother for having such a resilient child and for her own fortitude.

"Miss Henry, you are a saint."

"Saint's a machine can only do one thing," my mother winks. "I got more tricks than that."

I sit shivering in the middle of the boat, the dark taste of the river still in my mouth. John Yoder had loaned me a sweater—a dark green, practical sweater I would keep for years—because I'd been cold all morning. I sit in the folds of his sweater on the center bench, my hands between my knees, trying to keep myself from trembling. My thighs clenched around the aluminum bench I try not to move.

I try not to look at the water, to imagine everything in the water and every living thing dead and alive the water has touched. I try not to catalog the contents of that fecal stew still in my mouth and lungs. I try to imagine something beyond the damp, swampy smell of mud.

I keep my eyes above the horizon on the gray woolly clouds just beginning to break up, revealing the new skin of the sky above. It's better than staring into the bottom of the boat where murky water and mud slosh side to side.

I keep my eyes on the tops of the trees, the spiky branches reaching upward, swaying slightly in a sudden, cooler breeze. I close my eyes, imagining the solidity of the bed at the motel, the weight of the blankets on my body, the impersonal darkness of the room.

John Yoder and my mother are calling out, to the wrecked houses and twisted trees, but I don't call out. Secretly, I hope we find no one, no one who will rock the boat climbing in, no one who will sit across from me on the other bench to cry or talk. I hope there is no one to rescue and we will go home soon. I no longer want pancakes; I want the firmness of my refugee bed.

Somehow the day passes and thankfully, while other boats discover other survivors, we do not. My mother

and John Yoder begin to scribble notes about certain
houses and locations, so they'll know how to find them
again once the water recedes.

I sit very still and silent against the possibility that
the boat might tip and this time John Yoder wouldn't be
able to reach me quickly enough and this fear is never
stronger than when we approach the temporary dock at
the edge of the staging area and the promise of dry land.
In that moment, I am convinced the water will reach up
and close its arms around me again.

It isn't until the second night that I finally cry. My
mother and John Yoder are standing outside the room
on the cement pad before the door in the glow of neon
signs. I can't see them but I know they are there. I can't
hear them but I know they are talking. There is a thin
sliver of greenish light between the room and the door,
left open just in case I stir. There is a thin band of light
along the blank green wall by the bed. It is a motel in
Biloxi or Gulfport.

I don't know that I am crying. I think I am simply
shivering still. But the pillow is wet and my face is wet
and my body shakes with sobs which I bury in the pillow
so that the crack between the room and the door will not
widen and I smell a dirt floor, rich with clay and iron and
the dank, rotting vegetation of the jungle, and I remember
closing my eyes, years earlier, on a pallet in the corner of a
small hut in Central Africa as Constance sobs.

I'm five or six and we are following a tuberculosis
epidemic across Central Africa, hoping to stay ahead
of the disease. Every five days or so, we move further
into the continent, set up a new base, and put out the
call to the countryside to come in for vaccination. After
a day or so, a truck arrives with alcohol, syringes, and
vaccine. Constance delivers the injections to lines of
women, children, and occasionally men, outside the
door of our hut.

One afternoon, in some small, forgotten village, the
truck arrives, drops its cargo and continues down the

dusty, rutted road. When Constance opens the cartons later that evening in the lantern light on a low metal table, her hands rustle frantically among the packing straw. I can hear her knuckles banging the sides of the boxes as her breath grows short and tight, the straw whispering and rasping around her fingers.

The cartons are filled with junk: broken toys, transistor radio parts, pieces of old clocks. The actual supplies have been sold, or delivered to rebel fighters, or simply destroyed in some brief and personal anti-colonial protest.

She begins to curse under her breath and I retreat to the pallet. At six I know to stay out of her way. The curses are low and constant as she rifles each carton. In a moment, she abruptly stops, becoming quiet. She closes each box, stacking them on the floor by the door and as she stacks I can see her shoulders trembling, her breath coming short.

When she turns into the room, she isn't looking at me. She isn't looking at anything. Her breath catches in her throat with a gasp and a raking, keening sob emerges from deep in her body, a sob held there for so long that it has no history, erupting like a fact of nature. I've never heard anything like it. I push myself further into the corner, arms clutching my knees.

She cries for two hours without ceasing. She backs from the boxes by the door until she's stopped by the opposite wall, then her legs simply crumple beneath her and she slides to the floor and cries. Her hands are limp in her lap, her chin resting on her chest, except in the moments she raises it to keen again.

I have no plan. I've never seen her cry before and the sight of it terrifies me. It has never occurred to me there is a force in the world that might make my mother cry. I don't know what to do. I do nothing. I lie on my pallet on the other side of the room. I pretend to be asleep, but I can't close my eyes. Listening to her sob with my eyes closed brings the entire world into negation.

I keep my eyes on the flickering lamp. The dusky yellow light. The oily silhouettes thrown to the cinder block walls of the hut. The deep shadow of the table bisecting the wall. I don't sleep that night; I watch the shadows, listening to my mother cry, and when the crying ceases, I bunch my shirt into my fists hoping it will not begin again.

The next day, we drive into the closest, larger village where there is a telephone and she harangues anyone she can find on the other end of the line in a blue fury. She shouts, she curses, she threatens. Now and then her voice lowers to a conspiratorial whisper. Three days later, the original supplies arrive. None are missing, nothing is broken.

I never see my mother cry again.

By the third day, the water has begun to recede, but we still go out in the boat. This is the time for assessments of damage and priority. Already houses on slightly higher ground have drained, leaving a foot of mud and garbage inside, the history of the storm and its aftermath apparent by the water lines scarring the walls. It won't take long for the mold to bloom in the heat.

I sit in the middle again. I feel more settled in my skin but keep my eyes to the sky and treetops still. The water is quieter and in some places we can begin to see the roads and sidewalks, sludged in hard ripples of sand. The cars we pass leak as the water lowers around them.

My mother is in the bow with a legal pad, taking notes, and John Yoder calls out to her now and then. The neighborhood has been cleared of survivors, so there are fewer boats. Now, most of the work is in the staging area, or further back, caring for the saved, relocating them to shelters or relatives.

It takes me more than an hour to notice the birds. They have slowly crept back into the trees from their invisible hiding places. Their songs are tentative, almost ghostly; they're calling out to each other, checking in, getting the lay of the land, and something about the process reassures me. I find a hawk in the sky above us and keep my eyes on him as he circles and dips, riding the invisible thermal currents above me.

A boat approaches from a distance and John Yoder hails them. Two young Mennonite men who can't be much older than twenty, they cut their engine, their boat drifting toward ours. I know I'm feeling better when I don't flinch as the two bump together.

Aaron is twenty-one, from Pennsylvania, and Marlin is twenty-three from somewhere in Minnesota. They wear black trousers and white shirts with the traditional broad brim hats and it makes me wonder if John Yoder has ever in his life dressed this way. They are pimply, fresh-faced and eager to please, exultant when John Yoder gives them a task for the next few hours.

After a moment, Aaron turns toward me, introducing himself anew.

"You must be Abigail, right? I've heard about you and your mother for years."

He extends his broad, pale hand and I take it. His fingers close around mine for an instant then release me. I think I must be blushing, though it's difficult to tell in the heat.

"It's such a joy to finally meet you. We're so thankful for the work you have done."

Constance mutters something under her breath and I return Aaron's smile. Marlin is quiet in his part of the boat. It's obvious that Aaron is the talker. Within Aaron's smile, there is some kind of certainty, bland though it is, that calms me and I feel my own smile deepen, as if it has taken hold of me.

"We heard what happened the other day. The Lord is truly glorious. It brings such peace that He watches over us."

Aaron leans in closer to me, his fingers on my bare arm. "Perhaps, you'd like to pray with me. In gratitude and surrender."

And, just for a passing instant, I want to pray with him. I want to pray in gratitude and surrender.

Constance rustles at the bow of the boat but John Yoder is already deflecting the prayer with a brief, nearly invisible wave of his hand. "Thank you, Brother Aaron. . ."

I awaken in the dark, the lap of water against the side of the boat receding into dream. It's dark and I'm cold. I know I am not at home because Max is not beside me. There's a wide swath of graded darkness to my right that must be a window. The only thing I hear is the hum of the air conditioner and my own low breathing. I remember where I am, floating in a glass box in the Sudanese sky.

The last time I'd met John Yoder was a couple of years ago. He was in Baltimore for a conference. Even though we hadn't seen each other in nearly twenty years, he was much the same. The broad shoulders and large, strong hands. The clear, blue eyes now slightly damp. He sat across the small coffee shop table and he only wanted to know about me: about my work, my husband, my life, and I couldn't help but tell him everything and he smiled and nodded, occasionally patting my hand with his and he was so happy for me, so unremittingly happy for me that I felt more alive somehow, as if I had been brought into a deeper focus, as if someone had simply reached up, made a fine adjustment, and I was all at once more clear and well-drawn.

I don't know that I am crying. I think I am shivering in the cold. But the pillow is wet and my face is wet. I should never talk to my mother when I'm away from home and alone. In a moment, my body begins to shake with sobs. I don't hold them in; I've learned to let them come.

"All true difficulties are a gift from God," Aaron exclaims, joyfully raising his arms expansively. He waves to my mother and me. "May the Lord bless and keep you both."

My mother isn't looking at me. She's looking past me to Aaron and Marlin when they push their boat away from ours. I don't think they hear what she says next, as their motor has already whined to life.

"Pray for us all, boys. We're gonna need it," Constance calls to them as their boat pulls away, "'This world's a real clusterfuck of blessings.'"

ACKNOWLEDGMENTS

"The Reason the Dress Is Yellow" was first published in *storySouth*, Issue 36, Fall 2013

"Yield" was first published in *r.kv.r.y. magazine*, Fall 2012

"Currency" was first published in *Red Savina Review*, Spring 2016

"Forensics" was first published in *Blue Fifth Review*, September 2012

"Knife" was first published in *Red Savina Review*, Spring 2014

"Stalemate" was first published in *Siren Magazine*, Summer 2012

"Tiny, Impossible" was first published in *The Tishman Review*, Volume 2, Issue 4 as "Face"

"Sense of Place" was first published in *27 Views of Greensboro*, Eno Publishing, March 2015

"Devastation Tour" was first published in *december magazine*, Volume 28.2, Fall/Winter 2017

Steve Mitchell has published in the *Iron Horse Review*, *CRAFT Literary*, *Harpur Palate*, *entropy*, *december magazine*, *Southeast Review*, and *North Carolina Literary Review*, among others. *Cloud Diary* (a novel) was published in 2018 by C&R Press and *The Naming of Ghosts* (a short story collection) was published in 2013 by Press 53. He is a winner of the Curt Johnson Prose Prize, judged by Lily King, the Lorian Hemingway International Short Story Prize, and the Alex Albright Creative Nonfiction Prize. He's co-owner of Scuppernong Books in Greensboro, North Carolina, and Editor at Scuppernong Editions. Find him at: www.clouddiary.org

About the Cover Artist

Peter Tandlund is a web and graphic designer, mostly with interactive things. He's also a songwriter and musician in Trabant, a Swedish alternative pop band. You can find him on Instagram @petertandlund